Sicilian Gothic

◄

The Convergence of Carmelo and Nellie

Sicilian Gothic

The Convergence of Carmelo and Nellie

A novel based on the lives of my parents

by Mario Tosto

Published by MT Words

Also available as an audiobook

Dedication

This book is dedicated to my grandchildren:

Camden

Justin

Chris

Lindsey

Nick

Anna

Corey

Ben

and their parents

A Word About Words

There are some Italian words sprinkled into the story, especially in accounts of the earliest times. To me, they evoked the worlds of my parents and kept me in the mood. To translate each of them would be interruptive and tedious, and none are essential to understanding the meaning of the context in which they are used. If you're interested, look them up—I often used collinsdictionary.com—but be advised that some of these words may be a bit "spicy" for some palates. Don't be stymied by these. Just think of them as flakes of red pepper in the sauce.

Contents

Preface

The following preface gives some information on how this book came to be. But you can skip it and start reading at Chapter 1, The Castoff.

AFTER FLAILING AWAY for two years on a memoir, I'd grown tired of writing about myself. By 2018 it needed yet another rewrite. How tedious. Several work avoidance schemes later, I settled on breaking the beast into two smaller books, one for each side of my mid-life crisis. I figured that at least the tedium would be broken into two smaller and more bearable jobs. But after fiddling with it briefly, I gave up and put the whole project aside temporarily. Alas, I had become boring to myself.

Then the idea came to write about the time before me, a biography of my parents. Might it be a prequel to the memoir? Maybe. But there was such scant evidence about them, especially about my father, who didn't set foot in America until he was in his mid-twenties. And besides, Carmelo and Nellie, my parents, were among the least complicated people in the world, hardly heroic in the usual sense. They were as close to the earth as two Italian immigrant manual laborers in the first half of the twentieth century could be. I wouldn't call them bland, but how interesting were they? What about them, other than that they were my parents, would be appealing? What was their story?

Well, they didn't have a story until their arranged marriage, and what they had after that is not the kind of story I'm prepared to tell here—maybe in the memoir. Before their fateful marriage (I would not call it a "union"), what they had was a convergence of convenience. That convergence occurred on September 23, 1939, in the village of Mount Morris, in northwestern New York State, when Nellie Rose Cascio wed Carmelo (no middle name) Tosto. The first fruit of that convergence came four hundred and fifty-seven days later, on December 23, 1940, in the nearby city of

Batavia, when the author of this story was born.

Seventy-seven years after that, I set out to gather some facts about my parents that could be developed into what I thought would be a biography. Kickstarting with a couple of old tape-recorded interviews, letters, photos, and legal documents, I also called on present-day relatives and friends who shared helpful information.

And, of course, I had the internet and powerful search resources. These presented me with the ship manifests, immigration records, census reports, newspaper stories, oral histories, photos, and other artifacts from which I assembled a base of facts to which I could tie much of this narrative. Once I descended into the murk of time and roamed their worlds as a mute observer and gleaner, I came to a new appreciation for Carmelo and Nellie—much more than when they were physically with me on earth.

However, I still didn't have enough details, especially about my father, to constitute a normal biography. My solution was to assemble the disparate fragments of their individual stories with the connective tissue of fiction. This novel refers to people, places, and events that are products of my imagination, though based on factual research.

Even as a work of fiction, this story is anchored much as possible to documented facts, many of which are in the endnotes. Some notes will resonate most with my family. Some will add a dimension to the narrative. And some will distinguish between fact and fiction. I hope none are necessary to appreciate the story.

It's too late to tell my parents, as we would all like to be told, that their lives were meaningful, even remarkable. May this portrait serve as a touchstone for future generations, convincing them that while they are certainly as unique as we have taught them to believe themselves to be, they are also part of a wider-sweeping drama called family. Even humanity.

MT

1 ⋈ The Castoff

la Ruota –The Foundling's Wheel

1901—Wheel of misfortune

LUBRICATION was not a high priority for the proprietors of the *Ruota dei Proietti*, the "Foundling's Wheel."[1] That's why it screeched when in use, as if announcing its painful purpose. It wasn't exactly a "wheel," except that it rotated, much like a lazy Susan (though, to Italy's regret, it wasn't lazy enough). To cope with a nationwide crisis of abandoned infants, *la Ruota* had become a subtle but integral part of the architecture of most of Italy's churches, hospitals, convents, and orphanages.

Someone abandoning an infant would open the secluded street-side door, place the child on the shelf, turn the wailing wheel so that it now faced the inside, shut the outer door, pull a bell cord, and slink away.

In turn-of-the-twentieth-century Sicily, there could be many reasons to abandon a newborn infant, but the main ones were shame and poverty, and usually both. Shame, even in good times, is always a potent motivator. The Catholic Church institutionalized its abhorrence of rampant sexuality by sanctioning sex only within the governable (by Church and State) confines of marriage. Out-of-wedlock births were, by definition, proof of inexcusable sensuality, and worthy of shame and punishment. *La Ruota* enabled sinners to discreetly divest themselves of their bad fruit and resume respectable lives.

Economic depressions added extra incentive to the practice of abandoning an infant, even a "legitimate" one. The Italian economy was already in tatters from a series of assaults resulting from wars, political power struggles, escalating taxes, and the disruptions induced by literal upheavals in the earth from Sicily's cantankerous volcano, Mount Etna. With the government in disarray and pitifully unable to provide any semblance of order and stability, extreme poverty became widespread. Though Catholicism deemed every child a gift from God, a family stretched to the breaking point by these economic conditions could reasonably view a new mouth to feed as the definition of "too much of a good thing."

Often, the only compassionate choice was to give up a child so that it might have a better chance of survival outside of its original family. The likelihood of this was greatly enhanced by the widespread institution of *la Ruota*, which saved thousands of children from the previously common practice of drowning and other lethal forms of abandonment.[2]

Catania, Sicily—May 1901

THE BELL

Sister Mary Carmela[3] looked up from her breviary. She had only moments before settled in for a session of quiet contemplation after a hard day scrubbing the kitchen, so her body half-hoped someone else would get it. But she heard no footsteps along the corridor past her cell leading to the *Ruota*. Very well, then, a sign! Her eagerness to serve God and please her superiors helped pry her loose from that comfortable chair to fulfill her new duty as Receiver of Abandoned Infants. As she approached, a baby's muffled whimper confirmed her role. She opened the inner door and reached for her first *proietto* (castoff). A note folded inside the blanket read simply: "27 May. Please feed."[4]

She brought the infant to one of the wet nurses employed by the hospital for such a purpose.[5] The head of the Foundling Rescues department, Sister Mary Avelina,[6] swept in.

"Congratulations, Sister Carmela. You've managed to retrieve your first castaway without tripping and dropping him. He's cute. Maybe we should give him the name of *Primo*,[7] in honor of your first case."

"Uh, oh, well, yes, if you say—"

"Or *Fortunato*[8] because you didn't drop him."

"Whatever you think, Mother. You usually name the—"

"In due time, Sister, in due time. We will await God's disposition."

"Of course, Mother."

"For now, Sister Carmela, let's just call him 'Carmelo,' in honor of your first case.

Sister Carmela blushed.

"Oh! No, Mother. Don't name him after me. He is … a gift from God. Let him be known as the dear charge of my namesake—Our Lady of Mount Carmel."

"Fine."

"I shall pray that he be quickly placed with a family that will bring honor and praise to the Founder of our Order."

The receiving institution had wide leeway in assigning surnames to in-taken infants, often marking a momentary happenstance as a defining characteristic. For example, if the sun was shining and this impressed the person doing the naming, the child's last name might be *Splendente*.[9] Or if the child arrived at night during a full moon, the last name might be *Lunapiena*.[10] Or if someone knocked at the door at that moment the name might be *Tocca*.[11] And in cases of no inspiration, there was a list of names from which to draw regardless of any defining circumstance.

For little Carmelo, events would *quickly* provide a name.

Riposto, ten miles north of Catania

Time was running out for Mariano Grasso and his wife Maria Castorina.[12] Their male babies weren't surviving. Giuseppina, their first live birth, was three years old when her sister, Concettina, was born. The pregnancies in between, and before, were marked by masses for the dead, or simply private tears.

Mariano had wanted—needed—a son. It wasn't simply a personal preference; he was feeling pressure from the norms of his day. Men were cast as protectors so a family without males might be considered weak and vulnerable, deficient in an important way. With their string of male baby bad luck, and reproductive time running out, adoption was the next best thing. Fortunately, the foundling "hospital" right down the road had a new male arrival and it would be happy to make the transfer. The hospital was so impressed with how quickly a home had become available—often, foundlings spent years without being adopted—that they saw it as a sign of the name that should characterize their newest arrival.

The word *tosto* means *quickly*[13] so, newly born and newly named Carmelo Tosto became the first, and what turned out to be the only, son of Maria Castorina and Mariano Grasso.

In acknowledgment of their divine gift, they quickly baptized Carmelo in the nearby church of Maria Santissima del Carmelo.[14]

Fisherboy

NO LONGER A *PROIETTO* Carmelo was free to grow up learning his adoptive father's fishing trade, often accompanying Mariano on his quests for other marketable seafood. On calm days when the tide was out, he would maneuver a small flat-bottom boat alone in the shallows watching the rocky bottom for octopus. Spying one, he would dart his hand into the water, pull up the creature, and bite it between the eyes, killing it instantly—[15] a treat for tonight's table or salable inventory for the fishmonger.

As Carmelo grew older, he realized he occupied a special place in the family as the only son. He came to love and appreciate his parents, empathizing with the hardships of their poverty and grateful for their unconditional love for him. That's why, one day when he was eight years old, he was overwhelmed when they presented him with a pair of new shoes,[16] the culmination of a long period of scrimping and saving. He solemnly promised to guard the shoes zealously.

But sometimes, the precautions we take to safeguard something precious turn out to endanger that very thing.

One day, wanting to take maximum care of his new shoes so they wouldn't get wet, dirty, or stolen, Carmelo buried them in the sand on the beach near their house. But later when he went to retrieve the shoes, he realized he'd forgotten where he had buried them. Or had someone taken them? Frantically searching up and down the beach and not finding the shoes, he burst into tears that would not stop as he confessed the loss to his parents, which he couldn't help but attribute to his own carelessness. Though the tears from his eyes eventually ceased, his heart was drenched with regret for many years afterward.

Identity

"WHY AM I 'TOSTO?'" No one else in this family has that name." [17]

Maria and Mariano knew it was a question he was bound to ask someday, but also a question that might reveal his ability to comprehend the answer. He was ten.[18]

"It was the name the hospital gave you when we took you home with us."

"Why is it different? I am Tosto, and you are Grasso."

Mariano looked to Maria, who looked back at Mariano. He cocked his head toward her.

"We adopted you," she said.

Carmelo had heard the term "adopted," and had a vague idea of what it meant. He had also heard the term "bastard," and knew it wasn't a good thing. Someone down by the boats had suggested the two terms were related.

"What does it mean that I am 'adopted'?"

"It means we have taken you into our family as one of us," Maria explained.

"But...but that means I'm not your son." Carmelo whimpered.

Mariano planted his finger firmly on the table top. "You are! You are as much my son as if ...as if this woman gave birth to you! As much as your sisters, Concettina and Giuseppina!"

No one moved for a long time.

Carmelo turned away and cautiously asked, "What happened to my...to ... to the woman who gave birth to me?"

Maria gently said, "We don't know."

"Who is she? Did she die?"

"We don't know," whispered his parents.

Carmelo turned back to face them.

"Why did you take me?"

"Because," said Maria, with a glance at her husband, "... because we wanted a son to love." She hugged him for a long time, then patted his head and said, "Now, go wash your face and get out there and mend some nets, Sonny boy!"

Often, adoptees feel a strong urge to connect with their birth parents. Not Carmelo. His appreciation for the life his adoptive family had given him, their love and sacrifice for him, stirred a corresponding resentment against his biological mother. He scoffed at a common legend meant to salvage some dignity for the *proietti*, that a child given up for adoption may have been born to royalty. In later years, he told his sister: "Even if she was a queen, I would not seek her. She refused me love but these people have raised me with the love and care that she didn't give."[19]

A wider workplace

CARMELO CONTINUED to mend nets, catch octopuses and tuna, enjoying the ever-present vastness of the sea until he was fourteen. It was then time for him to make a more substantial contribution to the economic life of his family. He needed a man's job. The Italian merchant marine had one for him. In the galley. From there he couldn't behold the sea as much as he would have liked, but the job paid much better than the sale of a few brain-bitten octopuses. Keeping only what he needed to survive, he sent most of his wages back to his parents in Riposto.[20]

A strong, reliable worker, Carmelo advanced through the ranks in the next few years, eventually ascending from the galley to the top deck. In time, he became a *marinaio scelto,*[21] an "able-bodied seaman" who often assisted in navigation.

Wider seas were now his workplace.

2 ⋈ Sick Transit

SS[22] *Venezia*

June 1910

FOR BARTOLOMEO CASCIO, the voyage had been grueling enough already. Just getting to the port of Palermo and onto the SS *Venezia*[23] was a daunting ordeal. At this moment, however, the strained hopes of Bartolomeo and his wife and two daughters were also at the mercy of a tiny bacterium in the body of their older daughter, three-year-old Francesca.

In 1910, scarlet fever was a leading cause of death among children. The only treatment was the passing of time. And good luck. That's why the feverish little girl, her mother, Giuseppa, and newborn sister, Natala, had been quarantined at one end of the ship, leaving Bartolomeo, their paterfamilias, anxious and powerless at the other end.[24]

Traveling by ship from Palermo to New York City in 1910 could take two weeks to a month in hot, smelly, bumpy, cramped quarters, and—illness notwithstanding—plenty of boredom. If Francesca's rash and sore throat didn't subside in that time, they all faced the same conditions on the way back to Palermo.

For Bartolomeo and his family, the momentous transition had started on June 10 as they bade goodbye to their home and their friends and neighbors in the village of Polizzi Generosa, about fifty miles southeast of Palermo. Though it was a sad leave-taking, everyone knew that moving to America was the best option available to their economically depressed community. Some were jealous Giuseppa had family already there who had helped make the arrangements, had even financed part of the trip. Others tried to be patient as they awaited their turn. Some Polizzis had even pitched in to finance the trip, hoping their generosity would be remembered—and reciprocated—when their *compari* took up residence on one of the streets of gold in America. Giuseppa's sister, Rosaria, had emigrated first about five years before, settling in the village of Mount Morris in western New York State, a village that apparently had not yet received its allotment of gilded thoroughfares.

Music man

PROCESSED AND ON BOARD, Bartolomeo and his fellow émigrés kept themselves distracted from the rigors of the journey by singing the old songs. Many of those within earshot would gather around him and sing to the accompaniment of his battered guitar. [25] It was one of the paltry few possessions they had managed to gather up for baggage on the *Venezia*. But it was the most awkward to pack so he simply carried it strapped to his back with a rope.

It was no paragon of the luthier's art, merely a cheap abandoned instrument he had picked up from a pile of trash on the outskirts of Polizzi during one of his regular hunts for firewood.[26] The guitar had been in bad shape and he had had to carefully glue parts of it back together in order to get it to sound anything like a musical instrument. But once functional, he found it magically easy to coax it into making music. A few consultations with village musicians pointed him to inner channels of inspiration that opened naturally to him and he started to sing along with the chords he banged out on the guitar.

The songs of the people were numerous, simple, and tasty as candy, and he had soon learned to toss them into any gathering and watch the music galvanize a random group into a boisterous, convivial glee club. His voice wasn't polished or especially pleasant, but his enthusiasm for the music and a strong rhythmic chording gave his audience a happy rallying point for their own voices. Everyone knew a song that evoked reminders of good times back in the Old Country, even the sad songs, and people quickly realized all they had to do was call out a title or a lyric phrase and Bartolomeo would reciprocate with at least a close approximation of the song. On the rare occasion when he didn't know a song, he asked to hear the tune and quickly came back with an acceptable response. When asked, "How do you know how a song is supposed to go if you haven't heard it before," he'd say, "I dunno. Most songs seem familiar to me somehow. I connect up a piece of one with a piece of another. Comes out all right most of the time."[27]

Between songfests, the passengers mostly talked.[28] They speculated about their new life should they survive this trip and eventual placement in their new homeland. They talked about their struggles to get on board this ship, the conditions of the homes they had left, the families that would surround them and teach them how to be Americans.

Small town genetics

HAD IT BEEN ANY OTHER YEAR, Bartolomeo Cascio and Giuseppa Giampapa would have brought a larger family, with at least two and maybe three or four other children in tow. But those other children hadn't lived long enough. Early death was common generally, but especially among the offspring of first cousins. In small Sicilian villages, inbreeding was common—understandably since it wasn't easy to find dates and meet potential mates who could add some healthy complexity to the gene pool. Bartolomeo and Giuseppa were first cousins,[29] so the deaths of most of their nine children were probably abetted by the genetic clashes common to the offspring of such inbreeding.

Francesca and Natala had somehow avoided the Cascio/Giampapa genetic booby traps but were now awaiting their fate from verdicts of the medical inspectors who would board the ship when it arrived close outside New York Harbor. If they, especially Francesca, were deemed healthy enough, the family would move north to Ellis Island for further processing as immigrants. But if any of them failed the medical inspections, they would face deportation even while in the shadow of the symbol of their hopes, The Statue of Liberty.

From her corner of the sickbay, Giuseppa prayed.

Mount Morris, New York

IT WAS A LARGE ROOM, but only one of two upstairs in the small house in the village of Mount Morris.[30] The bed was large, too. Its faded brass posts and ornamental filigrees mutely mocked the grandeur of a church organ. As she dusted the last of the glass figurines on the small dresser, Rosaria Trippi paused and prayed for her sister and family who were, God willing, on a ship somewhere out on the Atlantic heading her way. Remembering her own turbulent passage five years earlier, she paused a few seconds in silent prayer asking God to wrap her and her family in His protecting love. Then she gave a quick glance around the room, closed the door, and padded downstairs.

It was quiet for now. But soon the children would be home from an outing with their Aunt Mary. Rosaria loaded wood into the large cookstove, then sat for a while rehearsing her plans for the coming arrival and enjoying the brief period of quiet.

Soon, maybe as soon as tomorrow, her sister and family would be moving in. The two families had corresponded over the preceding months to make the arrangements for the Cascios to emigrate from Polizzi and start the long process of becoming citizens of the United States. "Rose," as she was now called by the locals, was proud to take her place in the long tradition of assisting families from the Old Country. Her own family had been aided by a different family with the same surname, Trippi, in the move from Sicily to America.[31] She felt right about it.

Her husband, Matteo, had gone to New York City with their eldest son, Joe, to escort the new arrivals back to Mount Morris and temporary lodging in their tiny house. Soon after, he would take Bartolomeo to work with him at "the railroad" and help him apply for a job. Compared to the meager work offerings in Polizzi, Mount Morris was a boom town where Bartolomeo would have his pick of jobs—as long as they involved only manual labor—if not on the "Delaware "Lackawan"[32] with Matteo, then in the salt mine, knitting mills, canning factories, or farms in the area.

Rose suddenly raised another prayer, that it would all be over with soon and she could have her house back. Though there was no discernible movement in her body, she knew a new life was stirring inside her.[33]

3 ⋈ Sea of Love

1915-1920

CARMELO'S ADVANCEMENT AS A SEAMAN was no doubt enhanced by his growing friendship with Enrico—"Rico"—Mancuso,[34] the ship's captain. It seemed an odd relationship: They were four or five years apart in age; Rico had education, training, and experience far beyond Carmelo's; he spoke at least three languages; could read and write; was sneaky and clever in ways that Carmelo couldn't imagine being. But he was from Catania, Carmelo's "home town" (as far as he knew), and exhibited an almost brotherly attachment for little[35] "Melo." Grateful for the guidance and protection offered by Rico, Carmelo tagged along on the older man's escapades as a buddy, but also as a lackey and confidante. Together they had explored almost every seaport in the Mediterranean, and beyond. Now they were steaming far to the northeast, almost to the Baltic, to a frequent stop, Constantinople. Rico often had "personal business" there, which he conducted while the ship was in port on company business.

Tüccar was a rich trader who often bought off-manifest items Rico had collected in his excursions around the world. They had also developed a friendship and over time Rico had become a welcome visitor to Tüccar's home. That's where he met Tüccar's eldest daughter, Ayla, with whom he fell in love. They had been seeing each other on every stay in Constantinople thereafter. It seemed a promising relationship, though it was not moving as quickly as Rico would have liked. There were still "cultural" issues to resolve, meaning he had yet to gain Tüccar's complete trust. Tüccar admitted to himself that Rico was indeed a cagey businessman, but he wondered how his deviousness would affect the trader's intimate circle. He allowed for his circumspection but decided to let time reveal what he should know.

During this stay, Rico's ship would be in port for at least two weeks, maybe three, not only to unload and take on new cargo but to perform repairs that couldn't be done while operational at sea. Rico invited Carmelo to accompany him for dinner at Tüccar's knowing that all who came to a Turkish family's home were welcome,. He hoped his green friend would make him look more substantial by comparison. Also, he hoped the novelty of his handsome little companion might provide enough distraction to allow Rico to steal a bit of private time with the trader in order to cultivate a closer relationship.

At dinner, as they sat on cushions at a low table helping themselves to all sorts of foods from a large platter, Carmelo admitted to himself that in Ayla, Rico had indeed taken to a lovely woman. And yet, he couldn't keep his eyes off Ayla's younger sister, Liomi,[36] who scintillated with wit and humor in addition to nearly blinding him with her beauty. For her part, Liomi seemed to find Carmelo fascinating as well—at least that's what he concluded from her penetrating looks and quick smile.

"Eat, my friend," said Tüccar. "Take another olive, have some bread. Don't be so shy."

Carmelo snapped to. He blushed, knowing he had looked stupefied as he stared at Liomi. He managed to get through the lavish meal without any more *faux pas*, and tried to engage in polite conversation with the others at the table—but he often lost his train of thought any time Liomi moved or spoke. At the end of the evening, Liomi cast a lingering eye on Carmelo as he and Rico departed. Carmelo nearly tripped backing out the door.

≈

ON THE WAY BACK to the ship, Carmelo couldn't stop talking about Liomi.

"She's something, eh, Rico?"

"Kind of flirty, I thought."

"You think? I mean, she seemed to like me."

"Why not? You're likable."

"Rico, I think I'm in love!"

"About time."

"Do you think she– I mean, could we–"

"*Caspita!*" Rico burst out. "You two almost stopped the dinner with your mooning! By the way, it was slick how you retrieved that olive from your lap —but it does leave a stain.

"Oh."

"Yes, Melo, she's available, and she's about your age. We'll be in port awhile. You're *Tosto*, so make your move quickly, *ragazzino!*"

"How...what do I...I should probably ask her father, right?"
"Absolutely! We'll be back at Tüccar's in a couple of days to do some business. Ask him then. Bring the valise."

"The valise?"

"You know, the one with the 'stuff' in it. From Tunis? Remember? Tüccar will appreciate that. It'll 'grease the skids.'"[37]

He laughed. Carmelo, after a beat, laughed also.

≈

Two days later, Carmelo's meeting with Tüccar went well. He was free to see Liomi socially, "as long as your intentions are honorable," Tüccar had said.

Honorable? It was incomprehensible to Carmelo that it be anything but. And it might have been even more than that. Was it sacrilegious to have this depth of feeling, this rapture, for another human being? He'd once had a strong—extremely strong—feeling while singing a hymn to the Madonna in church.[38] It was almost physical. His enchantment with Liomi was on that level.

Over the coming days, both within her presence and back on the ship, he increasingly lost sight of her mere humanity. She glowed in his soul like a divine being, separate from the coarseness of ordinary life, a magnificent exception, ruler of a world he was willing to die to enter. He thought to himself: "You are a captive, Carmelo, owned by a ravishing queen!"

Over the next two weeks, Carmelo and Liomi spent time with each other almost every day. They walked hand in hand all over Constantinople, seeing the sights, and finding quiet places to be with each other in relative privacy. Carmelo told her of his mysterious origins, his loving adoptive family, his ambitions to be a Navigator. She spoke of Turkish poets and balladeers, even singing him a popular song by Aşık Veysel, *Black Earth*[39]. She spoke of children and family. She told him of her love for him. Their bond grew as quickly as their time together ran out.

≈

TOO SOON, THE SHIP WAS READY to depart. It had stops in Tunis and ports west along the way and back.

"How long will you be gone?" she asked.

"Three months."

"Oh, such a long time. But, dear Carmelo, know this, I will wait for you. I will see no one else in the meantime. Will you do the same?"

"Being with you is all I hope for now."

"Write to me!" she said.

Carmelo blushed.

"I don't know how to write," he stammered. "I never went to school past third grade—I had to work with my father, even as a little kid. I never learned to read or write.[40] "

"Ah. Well, get the Captain to help. He's your friend, you say. It's simple: You just speak the words and he will write them down and send them to me in a letter."

"All right, I'll ask him."

On the day of departure, they kissed and embraced for a long time.

"I'm not going to wave goodbye, Carmelo," said Liomi. "Here's what I'm going to do, so you remember how we will stay in touch."

She raised her hand and gestured as if writing on the air with a pen.

"And now, you do it."

He raised his hand and then combined the writing gesture with a wave goodbye.

"Do not forget me," she whispered.

"Non ti scordar di me,[41]" he replied.

≈

RICO READILY AGREED to be Carmelo's scribe, not only out of friendship but as a way to keep tabs on this new factor in Tüccar's household. Though he'd tried for many months to ingratiate himself with Ayla's father, even plying him with gifts and elaborate expressions of respect, Tüccar was still hesitant to cross the line between business familiarity and familial intimacy. And yet, Rico noted, he'd been more quickly responsive to Carmelo. He was jealous of that. Was it his youth? His better looks? Even his naïveté? Did Rico's connections in Tunis portend a threat to

Tüccar? In the end, Rico consoled himself with the belief that their chemistry had not yet gelled. Whatever the reason, he intended to be Tüccar's son-in-law some day and he wasn't going to let this little lovesick *stronzo* get in the way.

Oblivious to Rico's wiles, Carmelo poured his heart into his letters, even quoting parts of an old Neapolitan love song: [42]

> *Non ti scordar di me!*
> *My life is bound up in you.*
> *I love you more and more,*
> *My dreams are always of you.*
> *My life is bound up in you.*

≈

WEEKS WENT BY BUT Liomi never wrote back. Carmelo wondered why. She certainly knew how to write—her wit alone revealed she was not only smart but had had some education. He rationalized that perhaps in that culture single women weren't allowed to correspond with a man without their father's permission. Or, had she forgotten him already? The rest of the song floated into his mind:

> *Do not forget me!*
> *My life is bound up in you.*
> *I love you more and more,*
> *My dreams are always of you.*
> *Do not forget me!*
> *My life is bound up in you.*
> *There will always be a nest in my heart for you.*
> *Do not forget me!*

≈

"RICO, WHY DOESN'T SHE write back?" Carmelo whined. "Have you posted my letters properly?"

Rico replied, "Yes, yes, stop fretting. She's playing hard to get. Women are like that. Show her that you're a loyal lover. Keep, the faith, Melo!"

"In the letters you get from him, does her father mention me?"

Rico started to speak, stopped, took a cigar out of a humidor and lit up, all the while studying Carmelo intently. Through the blue haze he said, "Tüccar, yes, Tüccar. Well, he's asked a few questions about you. Just the usual, about your background, your character, your other girlfriends—"

"What other girlfriends? I don't have any—"[43]

"Hey, hey, don't get so defensive! These are typical fatherly questions."

"And how did you answer them?" asked Carmelo.

Rico raised up a thumb. "You're all right, kid. Just cool down a bit. You're turning my cabin into a sauna!"

They both laughed.

More weeks passed, more ports passed, but Carmelo had only one port in mind: Constantinople next month. This time, he wouldn't hem and haw. He'd come right out and declare his marriage intentions to Tüccar. He could learn to be patient in the meantime if there could be some assurance they'd be together eventually.

≈

Some weeks later, in Tüccar's office

"MEHMED'S NOT RIGHT for me, Father," said Liomi through tears. "He's too old. He smells bad. He's fat. And he's from Georgia!"

Tüccar put down his pen and closed his ledgers. He said, "Georgia's a nice place. Lots of fine people come from Georgia. Important people. Like that up-and-coming Marxist, Ioseb Besarionis dze Jughashvili. He's from Georgia.

Liomi threw up her hands, wide-eyed, "What's that got to do with me? Mehmed's no Stalin. And he's not my type."

"Oh? What is your type, little one?"

"You know! You know!"

"That little sailor boy?"

"Carmelo. Yes! He's so gentle, so considerate."

Tüccar reached for her hand. She withdrew it.

"Precious jewel, but when he's away, he never writes to you. He never sends gifts. He doesn't try to stay in touch with you. He is invisible. How much could he care about you?"

Liomi slowly shook her head.

"I know. I know. He doesn't know how to write. Maybe Captain Mancuso won't do it for him, as I suggested. Maybe he's been sick. Oh! Maybe he's...dead!"

She burst into tears.

"I love him, Father. Now, he's disappeared. Why?"

Tüccar opened a lower drawer in his desk and took out some envelopes.

"I hear from Captain Mancuso, my friend and business partner now and then, and he never mentions anything as serious as your...your sailor boy coming to any harm. In fact, he complains about the boy staying out all night on shore leave."

Liomi sobbed, "No! Not my Carmelo. He's not that kind of—"

"I'm not saying that," replied Tüccar. "I meant he seems to be healthy and normal. Young men are easily distracted."

Liomi stared at the letters and pointed.

"What else does he say about Carmelo?"

Tüccar gathered the papers into his lap.

"Nothing," he said. "Very little. Just those couple of things. Just in passing. Rico mostly talks about business. And, of course, Ayla. He really wants to make a proposal about her."

Liomi rolled her eyes. "That guy! What an oaf. He's a crook! I've seen what he smuggles into this house."

Tüccar put the envelopes away. When he looked up, Liomi had left the room.

He opened the top drawer and withdrew a letter that had arrived only yesterday. It was from Rico. He re-read, for the tenth time, the part about Carmelo:

Now!

≈

Banishment

A FEW WEEKS LATER, Tüccar met the two seamen at the door. His eyes fixed on Carmelo standing behind the captain, holding a small valise. Carmelo smiled broadly. Tüccar glowered back.

"You!" he bellowed and pointed at Carmelo. "You are not allowed in my house. Leave! Now!"

He beckoned for Rico to enter but stepped forward blocking Carmelo, who had attempted to follow him.

"Excuse me?" said Carmelo. "What do you mean? What? Why —"[4]

He raised the valise. Tüccar snatched it out of his hand.

"Liomi will not see you!" growled Tüccar.

"Uh, well, I can come back anoth—"

"Not now, not ever. Leave, I say!"[45]

Carmelo threw up his hands, saying, "There must be some misunderstanding. I only—"

Tüccar lunged at him and Carmelo bolted.

≈

Back on the ship

IT TOOK A WEEK for Carmelo's hands and feet to heal. He had punched and kicked every inanimate object in his path back to the ship. But when he got to his berth, he buried his head under a pillow and sobbed. All night until morning.

But another meaning of *tosto* is *tough*,[46] which is why he worked that week despite his injuries. And he avoided Rico as much as possible. On the few occasions when they crossed paths, both were silent. His self-inflicted wounds, and his shame at having Rico see him ejected from Tüccar's home, rendered him dumbstruck.

Rico seemed to be avoiding him, too. They hardly spoke, except about work when absolutely necessary, and even then, he was uncharacteristically bossy and critical.

Their next port of call would be Mykonos, in the Aegean. It gave Carmelo plenty of time to wonder why his friend hadn't come to his rescue, hadn't at least tried to correct whatever misconception Tüccar might have had about him. Why had he slinked into the house without him? Why had their friendship suddenly grown cold, formal? When time and work dampened the embers of his shame and anger, they flared up again at his next unanswered "why?"

Sebastiano Grasso,[47] a deckhand who worked with him, and who also came from the Riposto area, noticed his tragic demeanor.

"You look like crap," he said. "What's wrong?"

"Nothing, Bas. Injuries. A fight."

"You look you're trying to recover from injuries to the soul, Melo. And it's not going well. Looks serious, my friend."

"Forget about it. Just thinking. Family things, mostly."

"Ah. Homesick?"

Resigning himself to Sebastiano's inability to take a hint, Carmelo replied, "Been a long time since I've seen them. Two years."

Sebastiano silently counted on his fingers then held up a hand. "Know what you mean. Four years for me. As long as we're on these floating villages, we'll probably never get back home."

Carmelo was not used to this kind of attention from a workmate. But Sebastiano's interest seemed sincere. He mentally filed away the encounter in case he should need a sounding board in other dilemmas.

4 ◄ Arrival

Approaching New York Harbor

June 23, 1910

"**NEW YORK! OVER THERE!**" someone shouted. No matter which language they spoke, everyone on board the *Venezia* that day understood the words, "New York."

Jammed up against the deck rails, the best they could see was a smudge on the horizon, land, and the prospect of having solid ground beneath their feet at last. But family and friends, and even the shipping company, had advised passengers that even so, the long voyage would not be over soon.

"Legalities. There are legalities, papers, lots of papers," someone had said.

One of the "legalities" was a seemingly endless series of health exams. Everyone had to undergo them, but Bartolomeo's family, and others who had either taken sick while on board or who had unreported preexisting conditions, had to go through even more.

At the quarantine gate

BARTOLOMEO STUDIED THE CROWD exiting the quarantine section, looking for his family. A squad of medical inspectors had clambered aboard the *Venezia* while it was still at sea, yet within sight of New York. He had seen some of them enter the quarantine section, where his wife and two daughters had been holed up for the past five days.[48]

At last, he saw them. Even at a height of 5'3"[49], Giuseppa stood out from many of the other women and children exiting the quarantine section. She cut a distinctive figure, with a swaddled baby held to her chest with one arm, and three-year-old Francesca attached to the other. Francesca carried a cloth bag that, though not large for an adult, she had to drag as she tried to keep up with her mother who was plowing through the crowd.

When Giuseppa spotted him, she called out, "Bartolo! Over here!" He turned and saw them, and made his way toward them beaming. "There you are! There you are! Oh! Oh! At last!"

When he reached them, he scooped up Francesca as he embraced his wife and infant. "I missed you. You were gone so long, so long. But now we're together again."

"Yes," she said. "So long apart. How are you?"

Bartolomeo looked to heaven, "Happy. Happy, good wife. Welcome to America!"

Giuseppa looked around the large room. "Not so fast, Bartolo," she said.

"What?" he asked. "Is there something wrong? Did the inspector...? How is the girl?" He stared closely at Francesca.

"She's fine. I meant it'll be a while till we're actually in America. There are more, more things to do..."

"Ah, legalities," he said knowingly.

"Yes, inspections, papers, waiting in line. I need to sit down and try to feed this baby. Find me a place."

Surveying the area, he led her to a bench filled with people. He smiled as he looked at a middle-aged man occupying an end spot.

"*Mi scusi, Signore,*" he said, cocking his head toward Giuseppa and the children. "My wife needs to sit for a little while. They just came from the quarantine...and the baby...she needs..."

The man said something in a language Bartolomeo didn't understand.[50]

"Please?" said Bartolomeo as he pointed to them.

The man glanced at Giuseppa, who bowed solemnly. He slowly rose and drifted into the crowd. Giuseppa sat and Francesca tried to climb onto her knee.

Bartolomeo squatted in front of them. "What did they say about the scarlet fever? Is she over it?"

"Yes, she's all right now," said Giuseppa. "But the inspectors get even more picky when we are almost there. Even if everything goes well for us, it will take a long time, more standing in line, more talks with inspectors." She swept her hand in a wide arc. "Thousands of people, only a few inspectors."

Bartolomeo shook his head. "No. Not thousands. Only about one thousand."

"More than that, still bad enough," she shot back.

With a horn blast resoundingly echoed by the pent-up hopes of its passengers, the *Venezia* turned north toward Ellis Island.

"I hear it's one more stop," said Bartolomeo. "Then we are in America."

Giuseppa shook her head slowly. "It's the worst stop, dear Bartolo. That's where they make the final decision, do you stay or do you go? For some, America, for some, Old Country again."

Bartolomeo patted his wife on the knee and rose. "I'll go take a look around. You rest."

"Take her," she said, indicating Francesca.

"I don't wanna go!" cried the child.

Giuseppa waved him away.

Out on the deck, he squeezed in beside a guy he recognized from the Palermo boarding.

"See anything yet?" he asked.

"Nope," his slightly annoyed neighbor replied. "Just keep looking in that direction."

They stared silently into the blue expanse for several minutes. "How long do you think it'll take to get there?" asked Bartolomeo. "To Ellis Island? I don't know but pretty close, I hear."

The ice broken, they continued to chat, sharing backgrounds, information they had gathered, gossiping, speculating on what lay ahead.

From the cabin deck above came a shout in English, "There she is!"

All eyes in steerage strained in tightened focus. Bartolomeo asked, "Over there? That little spot?"

"*Si, si,*" said the man. "The Statue."

"Of Liberty?"

"Yes, yes. Statue of Liberty. Almost to Ellis."

The crowd started to swirl as word spread and people tried to get a better view. Bartolomeo dashed back to get his family.

When they returned, Giuseppa exclaimed, "*Mamma mia!* She's huge! I've never seen a statue that big. Like a goddess."[51]

Bartolomeo pointed to the northwest as the tip of Manhattan slowly came into view, "America! We are here! We are home, Popina!"

Still awed by the bigness of everything looming before her, Giuseppa gestured a cross on her chest. "*Bella Madre* [beautiful mother]," she whispered.

Amid the chatter, she also breathed, "For the baby's sake I hope we make it in time."

Final approach

THE SHIP BEGAN ITS DOCKING MANEUVERS in New York Harbor. Soon its gates opened and cabin passengers streamed out and onto the pier. Those fortunate eighty would be ferried immediately to New York City. Then the ship would head toward Ellis Island where the barely-patient masses in steerage would be staged for transfer to the island and the enormous reception building. Immigration personnel, who spoke a variety of languages, were waiting to organize passengers into groups of thirty.

Bartolomeo adjusted the identification tags on his wife and daughters. Giuseppa adjusted his tag. He squatted in front of his older daughter and stabbed his finger at her ID tag.

"Francesca, do *not* take this tag off. Hear me? Do not take this tag off because if you do, you would get LOST. You would never see us again. *Capisci*?" The little girl nodded and clapped her hands over her tag.

Their group was finally led to the top deck of a waiting barge, their trunk in the baggage hold below. Soon they were at the pier and allowed to walk onto a surface that did not sway, even though their legs continued to make rebalancing adjustments as if still on board.

"Hang on to me, Barto," shouted Giuseppa. "I'm dizzy." "Yes. It's all right," he said. "You'll get used to it soon."

They staggered into the great reception hall, along with hundreds of fellow passengers. After some searching, they commandeered a small space for themselves where they could sit and watch the grand drama of American immigration processing.

The hall functioned as an outsized waiting room outside of a doctor's office[52]—in this case, several tiny "offices" out in the open consisting of only a stand and a high stool for the doctor. A steep stairway led up to the examination stand where doctors, each accompanied by an appropriate interpreter, performed the final medical exam, "The Two-Minute Special," as cynics called it.

If the stairway seemed steeper than necessary, it was purposely so. It was one of the means by which the immigrants were put through their first and most rigorous physical test. Scrutinizing the climbers from above, doctors looked for signs of weakness, heavy breathing (possibly indicative of heart problems), lameness, and even signs of mental imbalance.

At the inspection stand, they examined the hair, face, neck, and hands of every person. When the examiner noticed some condition that needed to be checked more thoroughly, he wrote with chalk a letter on the immigrant's clothes. An "X" high on the right shoulder alerted to possible mental defects. "B" meant back problems. "H" stood for heart problems. And so on.

Depending on the results of the exam, passengers would be released either to American soil, or to the deportation holding area.

≈

Big Al

AFTER OBSERVING THE SCENE for a long time, Bartolomeo bent to Giuseppa's ear and asked, "Ever heard of the '*al pisi*?'

"What?"

He whispered, "I heard if the inspectors catch you with it, you can't get off the ship. They send you back! I think it's some kind of disease."

"I have no idea," said Giuseppa, adjusting the shawl as she tried to nurse Natala. "Get me the supplement out of that bag. She's not getting enough from me."

"You eating enough? Are you? Remember, you've got to eat f–"

"I know, I know. I'm eating fine." Natala fussed.

"It's something about me, not making enough milk. Same old problem."

Bartolomeo shook his head. "No, not that. No more babies dying."

He retrieved the container, opened it, and handed it to Giuseppa. "Maybe in America they got doctors can fix that."

"*Caspita!*" He nudged Giuseppa and nodded toward a woman

limping past them. "Look," he whispered. "I think she's got whatever it is."

"Got what?"

"Yesterday, I saw her come from the inspector. She broke down crying and saying over and over, '*al pisi!* No *al pisi!* No!'"

Giuseppa eyed the young woman carefully.

"I never saw her in quarantine," she said. "Probably not a disease. Could be about the limp."

"What about it?" asked Bartolomeo.

"I don't know. It's too bad. Doesn't look good on a young person." They both stared dumbly at the woman while Giuseppa administered the supplement to Natala.

"Maybe it's not Italian, this *al pisi*," she said. "Maybe it's Arabic, or French."

"Whatever it is," said Bartolomeo, "it isn't good."

"Ask one of those interpreters that came on with the inspectors. We had an interpreter in the quarantine.[53]

"How was his Italian?" asked Bartolomeo.

"*Mezza mezza*," she replied. "Says he speaks fifteen languages. He asked me questions about the girl: how old, any other sickness, what's her name...like that. He seemed to understand me. He told me we were clean. Nice young man. Redhead. Name is 'Clam.' Or 'Clem,' I don't know for sure."

"It's a good idea, ask the interpreter," said Bartolomeo as he studied the vast room looking for a red-headed American.

"He told me we needed fumigation," she said.

"Huh?"

"I mean the clothes. They fumigate the clothes to kill bugs."

"Hmmm...I don't know about that. My clothes," he plucked at his shirt. "What do they do to your clothes?"

"Spray with some kind of gas."

"No. I didn't have fumigation. Clothes been on me the whole time."

"That's because you weren't sick. You weren't in the quarantine. Before we could come out, we had to take an infection bath, too. Some kind of colored water and stinky bar soap."

Bartolomeo leaned in and sniffed Giuseppa's dress. "I thought you smelled kind of funny."

She poked him and screwed up her face. "Was nasty. But the guy said we were 'as clean as a *fischetto*' afterwards. Must be a good thing because, *bella Madre*, I don't think I could have gone one more day in that hellhole."

He patted her on the back and smooched baby Natala. He bent to Francesca and asked, "Do you feel better?" She nodded and said, "I ate a banana."

Giuseppa patted her on the head. "They gave it for Natala but she couldn't eat it so I gave it to her."

He looked out over the crowd. "It'll be a long wait, but at least we've got each other for company. Some creepy characters out there."

"What are we waiting for?" Giuseppa asked.

"Waiting for our group to be called for inspection." He pointed to the stairway that led to the doctors sitting at high stools with the ship's manifest open in front of them.

"See those guys up there? We've got to pass their inspection before we can get our landing cards."

"Yes, I know" said Giuseppa.

"Mostly health," he replied. "It's a short inspection, but with so many people it takes a long time to get the whole bunch of us through."

He started to walk toward the staircase.

"Wait here," he called. "I'm going to scout around for a better place in line. Keep an eye on me. When I give you the signal, come to where I am and stick close to me."

Giuseppa tracked him as he sought a way up the staircase. She glanced to the upper level at the inspection stands and gasped.

"Bartolo!" she shouted, "he's there!" She waved toward the inspection area. "Up there! Next to the inspector, third one over."

Bartolomeo squinted as he scoured the swarm at the top of the stairs.

"Who's there?" he called back.

"The translator, the interpreter! The guy. Clam. He knows me. Talk to him."

Bartolomeo started forcing his way up, as though he had a message for the inspector.

"*Mi scusi*," he said breathlessly, as he writhed his way up the stairs. "Clam! *Messaggio per il Signore* Clam!"

Giuseppa watched his antics with a combination of horror and amusement. People didn't like being jostled and cut in front of. But Bartolomeo persisted and eventually made it to the Inspectors' Station. With wild and broad gestures, including darting looks back downstairs at his family, he gained the attention of a wiry red-headed man. They came to the railing and Bartolomeo pointed to Giuseppa. The redhead stared, then waved wanly at her. After a few seconds of conversation, Bartolomeo threw up his hands and returned dejectedly to the assembly room below.

"Well?" Giuseppa asked. "Did he remember me? Did he translate the—?"

Bartolomeo shook his head. "Not Clam. It's Clem."

"Good to know," she replied.

"Yes, he remembers you. And it's not *al pisi*."

Giuseppa waited.

"It's letters, just letters. Stands for words. Three letters: L, P, and C. He says it's on your record book." [54]

Giuseppa thought about it for a few seconds, then said, "L-P-C, LPC. Yes, I know it. I saw it on his ledger."

"And it's not a disease," he said.

"Yes, no, it's not. Not a disease."

"But it's serious. Could get us sent back."

"What did he say it means?"

Bartolomeo scratched his head. "Something Public Something. Means government has to take care of you. Like if you're too sick then they have to pay for your hospital and doctors and food and..."

"Oh, you mean like the dole?"

"Yes, something like that. Means government has to pay if you can't support yourself."

"Because you're too poor."

"Yeah, so they send you back and make the shipping company pay."

Giuseppa thought a moment. Then she said, "We're not getting sent back. We got the LPC because Francesca had the scarlet."

"How do you know we're not getting sent back?"

"Because the doctor, Bauer was his name[55], the inspector, said we were healthy enough. Because Francesca was cured and we didn't have any other problems that would make us charity on the government. I think LPC means 'possible charity case.' I don't know the *inglese* way to say it, but we're clean, we're clear to go. Bauer said it, and Cl— Clem told me in Italian we're clear to go."

A guard called out their group number. Bartolomeo eyed the staircase leading to the Registry Room. "Well then," he said, "we will soon find out if that's true."

Giuseppa sighed. At least she now had some help with the two children. Tired as she was, she nodded assent to his suggestion. "Here we go! Take the girl. Why did they make these steps so steep? It's almost like a ladder. Just getting up them will be a test in itself. If I don't make it, we're on the next ship to Palermo."

"We'll make it," said Bartolomeo. "Remember, Clem said you were healthy."

He took Francesca with one hand and offered his other hand to his wife. They joined the clot of immigrants oozing through the steep and narrow strait toward freedom. And home.

5 ⋈ Rumors of War

Statue of Christopher Columbus in Huelva, Spain

1925: Huelva, Spain

"What's with all the *rumore* in the harbor, Captain?" Sebastiano pointed to several spots where lumber was being unloaded and scaffolds were being laid out.

"The fuss? Ah, they're just starting the buildup for the big *festa*," said Captain Rico Mancuso. He and some of his deck crew were strolling along the wharf in Huelva, Spain. Refueling had been completed and the last of the supplies were being loaded on their freighter, the *Faleria*. "These Spaniards, they go *pazzo* celebrating Cristofero Colombo's departure for America in 1492. They do it every year. Starts in a couple weeks."

Sebastiano spat into the gutter. "Looks like a pretty big deal. Like a saint day. That some kind of grandstand over there?"

"Probably gonna be," said Rico. "Parades, speeches, fireworks— women!—day after day until August 3rd. They brag the 'New World' got discovered after our Genoese explorer launched from here. I saw a big banner: *Huelva: Gateway to the New World!* As if these local yokels had much to do with it. This is the last big port out of the Mediterranean, close outside Gibraltar. If you're going west, this is where you leave from no matter where you're going after that."

"Ah, location, location, location," quipped Sebastiano.

Rico snorted. "Sure, but more than that. Money. This is where the deal-making got started. This is where those local pirates, the Pinzón brothers, got their fingers in."

"Pirates put up the money?"

"Some. But the Spanish government put up most of it. The Pinzóns were in tight with Ferdinand. Isabella too."

Sebastiano frowned. "But pirates? Dangerous bunch to deal with."

"On the high seas maybe," said Rico. "But here in Huelva, they're respectable businessmen. All that stolen treasure can be turned into a shipping business– less risky. But hey, Colombo also had 'divine intervention,' my friend. The blessed Franciscans said a prayer or two in favor of the scheme."

"Huh?"

"I mean, they provided the 'safe harbor' for the Genoese to make his pitch. They gave him credibility with the government in Castile, made the introductions, gave the blessing—you know, prayer."

"Ah. Those little beggars[56] work in mysterious ways."

"Of course, the Pinzóns had ships to contribute to the cause."

They had reached the *Faleria*. Rico eyed it skeptically. She was only three years old, but homely as a turnip. She bore the same utilitarian mien as her twin sister, which had been configured as an oil tanker. He'd captained better-looking but older craft in his day, especially when he'd regularly tie up at the port of Constantinople—*Ahia!*[57] The memory unleashed a pang of regret. He'd been kicked out of the home of the man he'd been sure was going to be his father-in-law, Tüccar, the rich Turkish trader. Rico's patience had been stretched too thin waiting for progress in his courtship with the trader's daughter, Ayla, and foolishly had made a move on Liomi, her sister.[58]

"Big mistake," he thought. "She ratted on me to Tüccar and, *boom*, I have to take my business elsewhere."

Soon after, he had been mysteriously let go from the shipping company and had to find another vessel to command. That ship loomed in front of him now, loaded with ore[59] and headed for Baltimore in the United States.

He had been allowed by his new employer to assemble his own deck crew, men on whom he most closely depended for safe and accurate functioning of the ship. Sebastiano Grasso was his OS, Ordinary Seaman. For his Able Seaman, his *marinaio scelto*, Rico recruited his old friend, Carmelo Tosto.

Last night, Carmelo hadn't joined them when they went for one last sweep through Huelva's sailor-servicing enterprises. He'd stayed behind, checking the ship and playing cards with the skeleton crew. He still felt uncomfortable being around his nemesis, Rico, even after the offer of a good job crewing for him. This mixed blessing had come out of a chance meeting in the neighborhood of a brothel in Naples a couple of months before.

Naples (earlier)[60]

"MELO!" cried Rico. He jogged up the street toward Carmelo. "Hey, compare, did you get your money's worth in there?"

At the sound of that familiar voice, Carmelo turned around.

"Rico. Hi," he murmured. "Oh, suppose so."

He resumed walking. "And you?" he asked.

"Sailing, it's a lonely life. Especially for young stallones like us."

"What you up to these days, Captain? Still putting your ... 'vessel' into Constantinople?"

Rico clapped his arm around Carmelo's shoulder.

"Ah, my friend. Not exactly. I mean, no... Not at all... No."

"Did they catch you with the contraband? Did the daughter, what's her name? Did she reject you?"

"More the personal issues," he replied soberly, "not commercial. The daughter, Ayla, she was always 'willing' to spend time with me. But Tüccar got pissed off about something and... you know how he is... and he kicked me out—kind of the same way he did you."

"Not good son-in-law material?" asked Carmelo .

"Maybe something like that, I suppose. Maybe. Kind of. Dunno."

"Yeah, Tüccar can be suddenly hostile, mysteriously."

They walked in silence a while. Carmelo tried to appear nonchalant as he asked, "Did you happen to see the other girl, you know... the sister, the younger one?"

Rico exploded with laughter. "Ha! Yeah, what was her name? I'm sure you've forgotten, you lovesick stronzo . Your eyes still haven't uncrossed from the time Tüccar kicked your ass out of his house."

"Liomi," said Carmelo quietly. "Yes, I still can't figure out what happened there. We were getting along so— "

"She's a beauty, all right, Melo. Prettier than her sister, I'm afraid."

"Did she ever mention me? Did she ask...?" Tears started to pool in his eyes.

"Nope. Not a word. She's the kind of girl who runs hot and cold in an instant. One minute she's all 'come hither,' and the next, the door slams in your face."

Carmelo thought about that a moment, then said, "That's not the way I remember her. We had a good thing going. Even talked about marriage."

Rico shrugged. "Ah, women. Can't live with them, can't live without them, mostly can't live with them. What you gonna do?"

They walked along in silence again.

"I miss her," said Carmelo wistfully. "I still don't understand why—"

"*Basta with that,*" *shot back Rico.* "*She's a fickle* puttana*! Get over it!*"

His beefy arm blocked Carmelo's punch.

"*Hey! Hey! It's over, Melo. Grow up, kid. Get that angel out of your head. She's just human.*"

Carmelo strode away from him. "*She's not what you say, Rico. Something happened. Some kind of misunderstanding. Tüccar's mind was poisoned. By you, Rico? I...I don't want to talk about it. Now, leave me alone!*" *He jogged ahead.*

Rico caught up to him. "*Okay, Okay. Subject closed. It was a bad scene but it's in the past now. Subject closed.* Finito*!*"

Carmelo spat and waved him off. "*Go away, Rico. I don't want to talk to you, don't want to hang out with you. I thought you were my friend...*"

"*Hey, Melo. I am your friend, more than your friend. Listen. I'm sorry. Really sorry. I know it's a painful subject. But it's closed, like I said. We won't talk about it anymore.*"

Carmelo kept walking in silence.

Rico said, "*Where you working these days?*"

"*Not working much. Odd jobs is all,*" *he replied.*

They'd parted ways soon after the dust-up in Constantinople. Rico had been suddenly relieved of his duties as captain of the ship that made regular runs to that port. Carmelo had stayed aboard and sailed on to Naples where he'd been replaced by the new captain. Not willing to re-enter the galley, a big demotion, he'd wandered Naples looking to start a new life, a life without Liomi. But before getting on a new ship, he needed some land time. He decided to catch a job in the city and think over what he wanted to do with his life now that it had been so cruelly demolished by Tüccar and whatever mysterious forces had impelled him to banish Carmelo.

"*How'd you like to get back on the seas, Melo?*" *asked Rico.*

"*You know a ship that's hiring?*"

"*Indeed I do. Mine!*" *Rico replied.* "*I just took over the* Faleria *, big cargo ship out in the harbor. I could use a reliable* marinaio scelto. *You interested?*"

"*Working for you?*" *Carmelo asked.*

"Uh-huh. I can start you as an AB[61] , and maybe move you up to Navigator someday."

Though it had taken some time to acquire his land legs, Carmelo had not been completely comfortable away from the sea. He preferred steel under his feet, not dirt. And while working as an AB he would still be considered a 'rating,' that is, a sailor without an official certificate, it was still a more prestigious position than what most of the other sailors held. Besides, it was up on deck in the open air, not in the dankness below. And it paid much better.

There was this tricky "interpersonal" issue. Since the incident in Constantinople, he'd grown deeply suspicious of Rico and was still smarting from that latest crude remark about Liomi.

"We depart for Genoa in a couple of days," said Rico. "What do you think?"

Carmelo knew he wouldn't be missed the next day at his job sweeping out the brothel. And the vision of the open sea overwhelmed him now.

"Able Seaman, with a shot at Navigator?" he asked.

Rico nodded vigorously.

"And no more dirty talk about my ... my interests ... my—"

"Love life, yes. Just don't get all moon-faced about it on the job. I need a good deckhand who knows how to sling a mooring line and work the navigation gear. I need you to have a sharp eye on the stars in the sky, not the ones in your dreams."

"You know I can do it, Rico."

"Yes I do. But will *you do it, Melo? Will you come on board the* Faleria *tomorrow?"*

Carmelo extended his hand. "Yes, I'll be there. Thanks for the offer."

≈

June: Huelva

THEY HAD TAKEN ON A LOAD of manganese ore in Genoa and were ready to depart Huelva for Baltimore in the United States. Carmelo joined the rest of the crew on deck for final instructions from the captain. Afterward, he sat below with his old friend and countryman, Sebastiano Grasso, who had not made it to the meeting.

"So, Bas, how was it last night? All partied out?"

"Drank too much," mumbled Sebastiano. "Or the *grappa* was cut with something horrible. Hope these fireworks in my head go away by the time we launch. You want the rest of this?" indicating his barely-touched meal.

"Did he make a fool of himself again?"

"Captain? Of course! He's such a *cazzo*. Loud, pushy, belligerent. Good thing we were around him or the Second would be taking us out of port today. And conducting a burial at sea."

"What!" cried Carmelo. Then he saw Sebastiano was grinning and laughed. "Oh, I see. Just kidding. Or wishing!"

"Sometimes you take things too seriously, Mel."

"Maybe. Anyway, did you hear any world news while you were out raising hell?" Carmelo asked.

Sebastiano shook his head. "What?"

"News of the world."

"Are you kidding? How long since you've been on shore leave?"

"It came in on the Marconi today. Mussolini has declared himself a dictator."

"That's not news, Melo. He's been running Italy like a dictator since he got to power the past two or three years. You know, they say he's just trying to make Italy great again".[62]

"I liked it when we just had a king. Victor Emmanuel's a nice guy."[63]

"Nice guys don't automatically know how to run a country. Italy was a mess before *il Duce* swung the *fasces*[64]—people starving in the streets, broken down city governments, riots, strikes—Christ, the fucking railroads didn't run unless some union boss got paid off!"

Carmelo nodded, "True. A mess."

"My uncle couldn't take it anymore. Piled his family onto a train that worked—eventually—got on a ship and made it to *l'America* while he could."

"What? People could do that?" burst out Carmelo. "Just pick up and leave?"

Sebastiano clapped his hands over his temples. "Ah! Not so loud, Melo. I'm in a tender way here."

"Sorry," whispered Carmelo. "How did your uncle get away?"

Sebastiano lowered his head to the table, covered it with his arms, and moaned softly, "Not easy. Not very easy. Long and dangerous, expensive proposition. He had a little money and a lot of luck. Took the train to Palermo, shared some lire with the authorities, and got a place in steerage on a boat headed for New York."

Carmelo thought about that for a while, imagined how a countryman might have perceived *l'America* after having lived in troubled *l'italia* all his life. It must have been a shock. Were the streets really paved with gold? Was there work for everyone? Did the fucking trains run—

"Bring me little water, Melo?" pleaded Sebastiano from under his huddle.

Carmelo brought it. Sebastiano took a sip, then another, and then chugged the rest. He stared at Carmelo with bloodshot eyes. "You thinking about *l'America*?" he asked. Then burped.

"Your uncle, he made it? His family?"

Slowly, Sebastiano told the story[65] of how his uncle's family had survived the rough passage to New York and somehow connected with *compari*, countrymen, there. No, no golden streets, but jobs on the waterfront. And inland there were farms, big farms with lots of work, especially for people used to scratching barren Italian ground for a pittance.

"But we're different, Melo. We're men of the sea. We dig in water."

"That's true," said Carmelo. "Working on the water is all I've ever known. What kind of work could we get? The American Merchant

Marine, or the Navy?"

"Fat chance of that. The Americans are building up for war, and Italy could be one of their enemies."

"Right. We're sworn to the King."

"Bah, Victor Emmanuel's a wimp. Benito's fixing that. He made the fucking railroads— "

"Run on time," filled in Carmelo. "I know, I know. I still like Victor Emmanuel. He's a nice man. But *il Duce* is a wrecking ball. Could be a cure worse than the disease. There used to be elections and a government and all that. Radio says he just kicked out the parliament and called himself dictator of Italy."

"Hey, since when do you follow politics, Melo? I thought you didn't read the papers."

"Right, I don't read at all. But the news still comes out on the radio and street talk, and what I just heard scares me."

"What did you hear?"

"That merchant marines, like us, are going to be drafted into the military!"

"Us? You're kidding. Drafted? What do we know about fighting?"

"About as much as any new recruit, Bas. They train you. Beat you into a killing machine."

"That might work on the captain. Rico would make a good fighter. He's got the *cogliones* for that sort of thing. Me, I'd shit my pants and die on the first day of battle."

"Same here. I'm a lover not a fighter. And I've lost love, Bas, but not the rest of my mind. Some days I don't know which is worse, but for now I'll take my chances. No draft for me."

"What're you going to do about it?" asked Sebastiano. "You gonna be a draft dodger? In the end, get shot for treason, or get shot as a fighting *fascista*—amounts to the same."

Carmelo looked away and said, "I don't know, Bas. But I've been thinking."

6 ◢ Journeys End/Begin

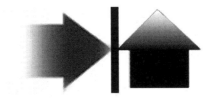

MATTEO MADE THE GESTURE for "what do you know?" His feet had complained from standing a long time at pier-side observing the humanity streaming out of the immigration building at Ellis Island. His son, Joe, checked the area again, turned from his observation post, drew his hands up to shoulder height and flipped his palms up. Nothing.

Matteo knew the last few steps into America would be slow and would feel even slower to seafaring immigrants enduring the final inspections—he'd experienced it himself five years before—but it was getting late and he didn't want to pay for another night in a hotel. He had train tickets for the two of them and the in-laws he had come to retrieve, but his cash was getting low. And so was his patience.

A short while later, a sharp whistle broke his reverie. Joe thought he had spotted them. Matteo rushed to his side. In the distance, he recognized his sister-in-law, Giuseppa. They were a ragged bunch, looking weary and wary as they ambled out of the building with dozens of others newly released to their fates on American soil.

He and Joe waved their arms and whistled, while Matteo called out, "Popina! Popina! Yo, Popina!" Giuseppa looked toward them, nudged Bartolomeo, smiled, and waved back. They moved toward each other. Their hugs and kisses and shouts of "Welcome" blended with the chorus of similar greetings in many languages.

After a quick update, they went to claim the baggage. Matteo motioned for Joe to pick up Francesca, who squirmed a bit, but quickly settled down under his flashy smile.

"You changed your money?" Matteo asked Bartolomeo.

"Yes,' he replied. "But I don't know what these monies mean."

Matteo laughed. "Don't worry, there's not much there, and it'll be gone soon. We've got to get you working right away!"

"Tomorrow?"

"Oh, no, no! Not tomorrow. Tomorrow you rest and take a look around your new home. Rose has made room for you at our house. For now, we've got to get to the train station. Come!"

"Rose?" asked Giuseppa.

"I'll explain later."

≈

Late that night in Mount Morris, New York

ROSE WAS AWAKENED by the sound of taxi doors slamming and exuberant chatter on the street below. She rushed downstairs and flew out the front door to greet her sister and her family.

Francesca lay groggily in Bartolomeo's arms while Natala whimpered in her mother's arms.

"Popina! Welcome to America!" she shouted. Only the family used Giuseppa's nickname.

They hugged and danced around each other.

"I keep hearing that," said Giuseppa, "so it must be true. We're here. At last!"

Rose took the baby, who immediately objected. She shooed the group into the house and sat them at the table. As they settled in, she brought out bread, butter, cheese, and water for refreshment.

Bartolomeo took a sip of the water. "Ha! Not like Polizzi water."

Matteo brought out a bottle of wine.[66] "Ah, your first taste of America, Bartolo! Sorry. Definitely not like Polizzi water. Not like Palermo water, or Catania, or even Cefalù water.[67]

Bartolomeo gently pushed aside the water glass. "Even if you go to Palermo, you bring your Polizzi water. You go to Cefalù, you bring your Polizzi water."

"Forget about Polizzi water," said Matteo. "In America, every city water is pretty much the same, not like in the Old Country where water comes from wells so it tastes like the land. Here we got 'treatment' water that comes from what they call a 'plant,' but not like a thing that grows in the ground. More like a factory. You get used to it. Here, Bartolo, here's something maybe more familiar? *Vino!*"

He had brought out two glasses and now poured some of the red wine into each.

"The baby needs milk," said Giuseppa.

"Dear, you can sit over there in that big chair," said Rose.

"She needs the supplement," said Giuseppa. "There's some in that bag over there."

Rose's expression darkened. "Are you...are you having the same... you know, 'production' problem?"

"Afraid so," said Giuseppa. "They gave us some of these supplements on the boat and that seems to be keeping her going. I don't think I can feed her all on my own."

"*Bella Madre*," whispered Rose. "Tomorrow we get more at the drug store."

"Thanks," said Giuseppa, a tear forming. "You've been so good to us. We couldn't have—"

"*Basta!*" said Rose. "It's what family does for family. The other Trippis[68] did a lot for us when we first came here. We're just doing our part."

Bartolomeo set down his glass. "Good *vino*, Matteo. No such luxury on that garbage scow, the *Venezia*."

Matteo poured him another. "You are with family now, and you will forget the hardships of the past weeks, Bartolo. After a little snack, Rose will show you to your room. And tomorrow, ah, well, tomorrow, I'm afraid I will have to leave you all here to have fun while I go off to work."

Bartolomeo said, "Yes, we will get ourselves organized and soon we will get work. Then we will get a place of our own and be out of your hair."

"Matteo will take you to the railroad office in a couple of days," said Rose. "They're always looking for strong young men like you, Bartolo. What are you, twenty-five?"

"Twenty-nine," he replied, "but yes, still strong enough to work hard!"

Matteo turned to Giuseppa. "Rose will take you to the drug store in the morning to get more food for the baby." He tapped Francesca on the shoulder, "And this big girl can have grown-up food, right?" Francesca lifted her head from her arms, opened her eyes, looked at her mother, nodded vaguely, and put her head back down. "Banana," she muttered.

"I have a question," said Bartolomeo. "You speak Italian but you used an *Americano* name for Rosaria. Rose? Why?"

Rose brought a glass of milk to Giuseppa and answered, "Ah! One of the first things you will learn here in America is that Americans have trouble with foreign words. Tangles up their tongues and they think they sound ridiculous and confused and stupid. They don't mind if others have trouble with their language, of course. And they like to shorten words, too, even your own name! So my Italian name is Rosaria, but that's too hard for people to say. So for years now I'm Rose—"

"And besides," added Matteo, "Rose is more *Americano*. And I think you like it, don't you? You fit in better."

"It's not bad," said Giuseppa. She laughed. "But I can't imagine what they will do to *Bar-to-lo-me-o!* Even I sometimes get tired of saying the whole thing and just say Bartolo."

Matteo offered, "Maybe Bart?

"Bart? I hope not," said Bartolomeo. "I hate the sound of it.

Maybe something else, huh?"

"Once you start mixing in with them," said Matteo, "you'll see how inventive they can be!"

"Plenty of time for that," said Rose. "But now, it's very late and Matteo has to get up soon for work. Come, let me show you to your room. Upstairs."

≈

Journeys begin

OVER THE FOLLOWING WEEKS, with the support of the Trippis and other family, the new immigrants started the slow process of assimilating into their new homeland. Though language difference posed an impediment, they were led along the same route their previous *compari* had taken to become Americanized. Bartolo soon found a place for his family on Eagle Street,[69] about twenty minutes away. Matteo guided him into steady work on the Pennsylvania Railroad and was his translator at the shops and government offices he needed to visit. Among the most urgent needs was to establish a reliable source of nourishment for Natala. Rose led the way, making contacts among the doctors and nurses she knew, and helping her sister shop at the drug and grocery stores.

Bartolomeo and Giuseppa took jobs while family and neighbors helped with childcare. The pay was meager, but every little bit helped. Even the children, when they got older, were expected to contribute to the income stream by turning their wages over to the family. But ultimately, Bartolomeo was the breadwinner—but soon everyone would know him as "Mike."

BartoloMike

THOUGH HE NEVER OFFICIALLY changed his name, no one, not even he, remembered when "Bartolomeo" became "Mike." Any five-syllable name was clumsy enough for his American coworkers, especially one in a foreign language. He tired of trying to teach them how to say it. Besides, he wanted to fit into his new homeland, and his long and awkward name was an impediment easily dispensed with in favor of something easier to say and more familiar to everyone. His new name might[71] have had something to do with his workplace.

The Railroad

> The Gandy Dancer is a railroad man
> And his work is never done
> With his pick and his shovel and his willing hands
> He makes the railroad run. [70]

Soon after they arrived in Mount Morris, Matteo Trippi had come through, as promised, and helped him get a job with "the Railroad." Several railroad companies had become established in the area over time and he worked for some of them including the Penn, the Erie & Lackawanna, and eventually the Delaware, Lackawanna and Western, referred to locally as the "Delaware Lackawan."

The work on a section crew was backbreaking, but he had a strong and willing back. He was given a large sledgehammer and told to look for loose spikes along the rails and bang them back into place. "Spike" was a word easy to understand. "Hey, spike over there," someone would shout, and motion for Bartolomeo to bash it. "Spike" was easy for Bartolomeo to say and "Mike" was a sound right next door, so imperceptibly Mike became his "working" name, and eventually his permanent, everyday American name. Everybody liked Mike. And he liked "Mike," too. So, "Mike" went from nickname to normal name.

One name he couldn't change was that of his job classification, *manual laborer*. That classification also stood for unskilled and probably illiterate. Also, expendable.

It was an era of furious railroad competition and expansion. As railroads merged, won, and lost routes, the effect on the laborers was not considered. Jobs were created and jobs were eliminated and those who did the basest of work were never a factor. Manual labor was cheap and readily available, and easily replaceable in the interest of larger corporate concerns. Mike was just a chip in the game. Within five years he lost and regained jobs on the railroad, filling in the gaps with the humblest tasks in other industries. He and his cohort—the immigrant Italians who resided on the "wrong" side of Mount Morris—were always on the edge of economic disaster.

In addition to spikes, Mike slammed a pick or a shovel into rocky railroad beds, lugged heavy wooden ties, and did the most menial of tasks. For these he was paid what at first looked to him like a small fortune each week: a dollar a day. He had been used to much less in the Old Country. Though he quickly discerned that the streets of America were more likely to be lined with garbage than gold, a strong but uneducated and unskilled worker could earn a comparatively more substantial sum merely for picking up that garbage. Railroad work was a class above that.

And while the wages were higher than in his hometown, Polizzi Generosa, so was the cost of living in Mount Morris. But now in America, he was head of his own economic workforce. With a wife (between pregnancies) and two daughters, and in a few years a son, the whole family could earn enough to afford a modest house and a few amenities in the marginalized, mostly immigrant, section of Mount Morris.

His neighborhood included many relatives and *compari*. A developer had bought a long strip of land along what eventually became North Main Street, and built several houses on it.[72] It was common for many of Mike's relatives, friends, and other Italians to eventually populate most of these houses, as immigrants tended to cluster.

Salt-ernative employment

FROM ROMAN TIMES, a salt mine was more than the worst workplace for a disposable work force, it was often where prisoners of war were worked to death. Its notoriety was such that even in later centuries, even when working conditions were less egregious, to describe any job as a "salt mine" was a euphemism for a one that is unpleasant, arduous, or repetitive.

Though railroad work was plentiful when he'd arrived.[73] everything changed when the Great Depression hit. Mike eventually lost his job as his employer merged with another company and reduced its workforce. Fortunately for his economic interests, there was other work for an unemployed unskilled laborer in the Mount Morris area. A few miles from Mount Morris, in the town of Retsof, [74] a salt mine had become a life line. Mike and Matteo went to work there.

It was probably while working at the mine that Mike's hair turned white. Most likely it was a coincidence, a natural phase of the aging process. Or was the process accelerated by the work itself? When he was assigned to the salt caverns a thousand feet below ground, using the "room and pillar"[75] method of harvesting salt meant he was surrounded by the whiteness of the walls, ceiling, and floor. And when he worked in the bagging area, the air was white with salt dust. It was some consolation that he got to work in a place not exposed to the harsh western New York winter weather. In a sense, it was "indoor" work, tedious but dry and room-temperature cool.

Social life

ST. PATRICK'S CATHOLIC CHURCH provided a meeting place and spiritual center for the large Italian population of Mount Morris. Even so, they never felt completely at home there, as it had been considered an Irish church long before they arrived. Sensitive their need, their rector, the noted theologian, Rev. Andrew Breen, arranged to bring an Italian immigrant, Salvatore Colonna, to the church as an assistant pastor. This gave the Italian community a sense of solidarity, even as many dreamed of having their own church. Their dream was realized four years later with the construction of The Church of the Assumption on Clinton Street.[76]

With work, or the search for work, occupying most of their time, socializing in the Mount Morris Italian community was limited to church activities and family gatherings now and then. But family gatherings were, in effect, block parties since such a large number of Mike's relatives and *compari* from the Old Country lived side by side on that several-block stretch of Main Street.

Religious feast days provided occasions for gatherings. In good times, the celebrations were laden with food, most of it traditional fare.

The most lavish feast was the St. Joseph's Table[77] on March 19. It centered on food because the legend that prompted it was about a miraculous relief from famine in answer to prayers to St. Joseph. According to legend, in thanksgiving, a community-wide celebration was held where wealthier citizens hosted an enormous buffet to which everyone, especially the poor and the sick, were invited. The practice was adopted in some form throughout Sicily and was imported to America with its immigrants.

Typically, on the feast day, one of the families would hold an open house, with help from neighbors. For days ahead, the kitchens in the neighborhood turned out a bewildering cornucopia of traditional foods including *sfinge, cannoli,* and *struffoli* (honeyballs.) Vegetable dishes included *cardune* (burdock), eggplant, and beans—especially the fava bean, which symbolized the harshness of the time when people were forced to eat what had been previously considered cattle fodder. The host family usually provided the fish and seafood entrees but no meat since the feast occurs during Lent. And, conveniently, there was *vino* in honor of the biblical story of the marriage feast at Cana. (Or simply because *vino* was *vino*, and tasted better than the local "plant" water.)

As ever, weddings also provided an opportunity for people to gather and relieve the burdens of everyday life for a few hours of gaiety and conviviality. At the other end of the spectrum, funerals also provided opportunities for social engagement, albeit with a more subdued tone. Wakes for the dead were usually held in homes, and people paid their respects in front of an open coffin. But there would always be food, drink, and gossip.

Daily life

THOUGH LATER GENERATIONS might find the living conditions at 63 North Main Street, where Mike's family eventually settled,[78] bordering on the outrageous, it was sufficient for the early occupants of that humble house that they had a home, some amenities, and a rich social environment where they could feel acceptance, love, and support. Though they often pined for many of the traditions and amenities of the Old Country, they knew they were immeasurably better off right where they were: in the immigrant section of the poor part of a tiny village in the western part of New York State, America.

 One of the family's prized possessions, acquired from Rose was a large wood-burning stove that dominated the kitchen. It was a far cry from the braziers of Polizzi,[80] which were mainly used for warmth, though at times, simple cooking was done on a grill placed above the charcoal embers. The behemoth in the Cascio kitchen was a far more versatile apparatus. It had cast iron cook tops with removable iron lids through which fresh firewood could be introduced. It even had an oven, and was also used in winter to provide extra wamth.

In time, an "ice box"[81] appeared, a precursor to electric

refrigerators that would become one of the essential elements of any modern kitchen.

Assimilation

THOUGH HIS IMMEDIATE FAMILY often beheld Mike as a stern tyrant, they were encased with him in the patriarchal culture of Sicily—and to a large extent, America, at the time—so they had few options. Tears and cries of physical and psychic anguish were a natural part of their way of life, like heavy workloads, discrimination, inconvenience, and near-poverty. Their brand of happiness was grittier than that of the *Americanos* in the other parts of town, but it seemed reasonable enough. Love was not unknown in their home, but harshness and insult were part of the deal.

They soon forgot the old days, but traces of the old ways remained. Yes, Sicily was in their bones, but American culture soon pervaded every aspect of their lives. Bent on providing the best they could for themselves, these recent Sicilians, entered the ranks of an emerging new subculture. They became solid Sicilian-Americans.

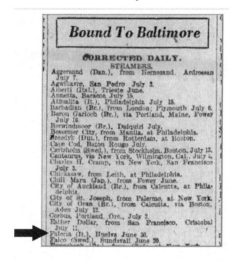

The Baltimore Sun July 16, 1925

```
"Bound to Baltimore ...
Faleria (It.), Huelva June 30"
```

July 1925 mid-ocean aboard the Faleria

Christopher Columbus would not have recognized the America of 1925. For one thing, there was no harbor on the island where he landed, two thousand miles to the south—and four hundred and thirty-three years earlier. For another, his ships were powered by wind and not by diesel oil. Like Columbus, Carmelo first glimpsed the New World after a sea voyage from Huelva, Spain, having previously departed from Genoa. But to twenty-four-year-old Carmelo Tosto, the scene was boringly familiar. All harbors looked much the same when the ships he worked on came into port, everyone's attention being focused on the delicate dance of moving a huge vessel into its berth.

Like Columbus, Carmelo contemplated the possibilities of this "New World," far in distance and culture from his native Italy and its brash new leader. He'd been greatly disturbed when he heard that merchant marine sailors like him would be drafted into military service. Rumors of war were rampant on the Continent, and many Italians were apprehensive about which side Italy would take in the looming conflicts. The sailors knew it didn't matter, they'd be targets in either case.

Since the heartbreak in Constantinople,[82] Carmelo had taken some comfort from the fact that Sebastiano Grasso, whom he called "Bas," had shown himself to be an empathetic and loyal friend, so much so that Carmelo had recommended him when Rico was assembling his crew for the *Faleria*. Together they had been dreaming about a route, not to India, but to freedom from Mussolini. Maybe Baltimore could be their Salvador.[83]

"I could try to contact my uncle in New York," said Sebastiano. "Maybe he could help us."

"When are you going to do that? We're in the middle of the ocean."

Sebastiano took out a map from a nearby drawer. He unrolled it, leaned in, and pointed to a spot on the map. "Right there. That's it," he said. "New York. Couple hundred miles from Baltimore."

"How would we get there?" asked Carmelo.

"How the hell should I know? I'm just saying I've got family a couple hundred miles from where we'll be docked. Getting there is half the fun, Melo!"

"Just getting off this ship will be twice the fun as that!"

"What do you mean? We get shore leave when we tie up at Baltimore, don't we? We just walk off and don't come back, bing-bing."

Carmelo shook his head. "That could be hard to pull off. Captain says he wants to get down to Tampa as soon as possible to pick up a load. "

"Yeah, but there's gotta be some downtime for us deck crew, even just an afternoon. We'll be in port at least a day. There's the manganese to unload, then that bad fuel tank needs to be flushed out, take on some ballast, and all the other prep."

"Yeah, and that's normally work for the other guys," said Carmelo, "but our team'll get pushed into service to make the turnaround quicker. I'm counting on it."

The bell sounded, ending their break. They put away the playing cards and gathered up the trash.

"We've got to think of something," said Sebastiano. "It's our only chance to get out of being cannon fodder for Benito."

"Once we figure out how to jump ship in Baltimore, maybe the Americans would take us in," replied Carmelo. "We could say we're refugees from a mad dictator."

"Easier said than done, Melo. Keep thinking!"

"Oh, I've never stopped, Bas."

8 ◄ Sisterhood

Frances & Nellie

c. 1923

"OW! YOU'RE PULLING MY HAIR!"

"Sit still, little sister. It's full of tangles."

Frances yanked the comb again.

"Owie! You're doing that on purpose."

"I am *not*." Frances gave another tug.

"Yes, you are! Ma!"

Josephine poked her head out of the doorway. Nellie sat on the ground at the edge of the open-air porch off the kitchen with her back to Frances, who was dragging a brush through her black hair.

84

"Natala, stop complaining. Francesca is doing you a favor. You whine like some kind of princess."

(Even though the family had Americanized their names— *Giuseppa* became Josephine, *Bartolomeo* became Mike, *Francesca* became simply Frances, and everyone came to know *Natala* as Nellie—at home and among the family, their mother tended to use the Italian names she had given them.)

"Come Monday," said Frances, 'you'll have to brush your own hair, kiddo."

Monday would be more than a grooming milestone. As today would be her last day of school, on Monday Frances would start work at the knitting mill in nearby Perry.[85] The timing was bad for her education. She was at last starting to get the hang of English and another year in school would have helped her fit in better with girls her age who were more Americanized. But the family needed income and she was the oldest child and now eligible to work. But that didn't mean she liked it that her little sister got to stay in school. True, Nellie was only fourteen and too young for the Mill and still worked part-time in the fields topping beets and picking string beans. It seemed somehow unfair, but she couldn't say exactly how or why.

"She's mad because she has to quit school," whimpered Nellie.

As she ducked back inside, Josephine said, "You'll get your turn soon enough, Natala."

Schooling for his children wasn't a high priority for Mike. It was a handy place to park kids while the older family members were away working. Having escaped his native Sicily before complete starvation had set in and killed off the rest of his family, he was only interested in meeting immediate needs. He expected everyone in the family to work as soon as they were able. Schooling as a preparation for a future life was barely comprehensible to him. Children were fun now and then but always expensive to maintain. They should be expected to pay some part of their way.

His wife disagreed but kept it to herself.[86] There were certain things worth striving for other than a paycheck. Like holiness. While she did her best to maintain a personal connection with God and the saints, she knew she could never attain the blessed state of complete dedication she desired. She was locked into a secular life, married and subservient to a man, bearing his children year after year, and between-times working to bring in some money. To her mind, the closest thing to living a spiritual life and a making a living was working in a convent. Her mother had done it.[87] But that kind of work was far out of reach for her now as a woman living in America, far from her homeland, far from the convents that would provide the opportunities to simultaneously work in the spiritual and secular economies.

She assumed that the highest human work was in the Church. And that the highest occupation for a woman in the Church was as a member of a religious community of women, living under vows of poverty, chastity, and obedience. While Josephine couldn't be a nun, she could produce daughters who might someday join the sisterhood. Many Italian families had the same aspiration. But at this point, only one of her two daughters was a likely candidate for that holy role. Though it was technically possible for Francesca to take the veil, it was highly unlikely. Not only did she not have the temperament or upbringing that would draw her to the religious community, life, even in humble Mount Morris, was hard enough that she could never escape from secular employment.

On the other hand, Josephine thought Natala might have been pre-ordained for that blessed vocation. She'd been named after Josephine's mother, who, though she worked as only a kitchen helper,[88] a decidedly secular task, she was able to do it within the context of a what she considered a holy institution, a convent.

Natala wept with joy when Josephine explained the holy vocation of a nun. "Yes, it is a life of deep love for God and all His creations. It's a life where everything is done for love, the purest love. No spot of sin can touch your soul, none of the dirty stuff we have to put up with on earth. No cursing, no anger, no killing, no hate. But no marriage, no children, no family life outside of the religious community of the convent. It's a great sacrifice, but for women who really want to be good, the best they can be, it's the way into heaven, where you can live forever next to the sacred heart of Jesus."

"I want to be a nun!" cried Natala through tears of overwhelming reverence and desire.

"Then you are going to have to be very, very good and pray to Jesus to be shown the way."

"I will!" cried Natala. "I'll pray and be good every day."

Josephine smiled knowingly. "Yes, that's what you must do. And that means no fighting with your sister, do you hear?"

Otherwise engaged

IT WAS NELLIE'S LAST week of school. Eighth grade would soon be over and her classmates were excited about going into high school in the fall, the public school nearby on Chapel Street, joining the other kids in the village and surrounding towns. Nellie would not be among them.

"Because it's not a Catholic school,"[89] she explained to her classmate, Teresa. "If the teachers aren't consecrated nuns, they might teach me things that would lead me away from my vocation."

Her friend rolled her eyes. "Are you still thinking of being a nun, Nellie? Haven't you noticed—" she stage-whispered, "...boys?"

"I don't care about that. I'm going to be a nun. It's a holy work and I'm going to keep my mind pure for that."

"Sounds boring."

"To you, maybe. Not to me."

"Aren't you going to get married and have kids?"

Nellie took a card out of her book bag and smiled warmly at it. "I'm already engaged."

"Huh? You're what? Only thirteen, fourteen? Do your parents...?" Nellie, flipped the card around so her friend could see it.

"Jesus!" Teresa gasped.

"Yes, him! Do you remember the story Sister Leonarda told from the Bible? About the wise and the foolish virgins?"

"Nope."

"The virgins were supposed to get ready to marry the bridegroom, Jesus."

"How many wives could he have?" asked Teresa.

"I don't know. He was Jesus, so I suppose he could have as many as he wanted," Nellie replied. "Some of the virgins got tired of their sacred duties and fell asleep. But the others kept on praying and having faith and keeping themselves inspired. So while the foolish virgins—"

"Please don't keep using that word."

"...so while the foolish ... women slept, the bridegroom came and he went off with the ones who kept themselves pure and alert and full of holy thoughts."

Glancing around to see if any nuns were in earshot, Teresa pushed the card away. "You realize, don't you, that that's just a story, just a what they call a 'parable?' It's all phonus balonus."[90]

As Nellie put the card away, she snapped, "Watch your language! Don't blaspheme."

"All right, Mrs. Grundy![91] Waste your life any way you want. Now that I think about it, you'd be a pretty good nun. Like sourpussus Leonarda-cussus ."

"Oh, Terrie, I feel sorry for you, because you're so disrespectful of God and His faithful ones. I'm quite afraid for your soul."

Teresa flounced off, chuckling, "Okie-dokie, Nellie-okie. We'll see how it goes."

9 ⋈ Plans Afoot

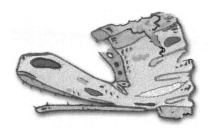

"HEY BAS, WHERE'S THAT OTHER WRENCH?"

Carmelo was rummaging through the tool locker. "Supposed to be two, but there's only one."

"What wrench?"

"The one for tightening the fuel tank valve cap. The little one. You had it yesterday."

Sebastiano sidled up to him, reached in his pocket and pulled out a wrench.

"You mean, this one?"

"Yeah."

"I put it away for safekeeping."

"In your pocket?"

"Safest place on the ship."

"How so?"

Sebastiano pulled him to one side. "Might be part of a plan, *compare*. We'll be in the Baltimore port tomorrow and I've been thinking how we can get off this tub even while everyone is under close scrutiny."

"Me, too," replied Carmelo. "You first. What's your plan?"

"Remember that trouble with a fuel tank a few days ago?"

"I remember we had to switch tanks because one of them got

plugged up. Lost half a day from that."

"Yeah, that one. Must have taken on some slimy diesel[92] in Huelva. He was pissed about that."

"Rico's always pissed about something. Anyway, what's your plan?"

"So, in port everybody's going to be busy. While the American stevedores unload the cargo, Captain says we're going to be flushing that bad tank before taking on fresh diesel."

"He knows that's illegal," said Carmelo. "Flushing tanks is supposed to be done only at sea only. It's not just the mess, it's dangerous, too. You know how fumes build up in those tanks.

"Oh, yeah."

"Hey ... you're not going to blow it up, are you?"

"What, and get some poor *marinaio* killed?" Sebastiano shot back, "Jesus, Melo, what kind of—"

Carmelo held up his hands. "All right. Just wanted to be sure you hadn't tripped on those shitty shoes of yours and hit your head on something and gone *pazzo*. So what's that little valve wrench got to do with—"

"What's my *shoes* got to do with *anything*? You got some kind of fetish?"

"No," said Carmelo in a soft voice, "I've always thought shoes should be taken care of." He pointed to the wrench. "Anyway, how is that wrench going to get us off this ship?"

"The drainage valves," said Sebastiano, "they got covers, to keep the diesel from leaking. If a cover isn't bolted down nice and tight, the tank leaks. *Capisci*? This little guy"—he flashed the wrench —"slips in under the valve cap and keeps it from closing all the way. I already checked it out.[93] It's a slow leak, but steady enough to be noticeable."

"And *illegal*, Bas! The *Americanos* won't like us dumping oil into their harbor. They'll come and arrest us, and—"

"What would they want with *stronzi* like you and me, Melo?

They'll go for Captain Fat Ass. They'll swamp him with accusations and paperwork. Maybe they'll arrest him. Maybe they'll seize the ship!"

"And why is that a good thing?"

"Distraction! Major distraction! Captain takes his eye off us, and we skip out bing-bing."

Carmelo shook his head. "Sounds pretty risky to me, Bas. Police'll be hanging around the ship. You think we're gonna slip away while they're not looking? Ha! They'll have guards posted at all the exits."

Sebastiano thought about it a moment. "You think?"

Carmelo drilled him with a look.

"Yeah, well, maybe. Okay, maybe not such a good plan." Sebastiano grinned. "But it would be fun to see him dragged off the ship, eh?"

"And maybe his crew, too. No, thanks, Bas. Going from this makeshift troop carrier to an American jail isn't really an improvement. And it'll never get us to your uncle's."

Sebastiano pointed at Carmelo.

"So, what do you suggest? Sweet talk *il Comandante*? Plant a big wet kiss on his big greasy lips? You know he's waiting on orders from *il Duce* to turn us into chum for submarines."

Carmelo stared at Sebastiano's feet.

"And speaking of garbage, I've noticed you've been tripping around in those ... shoes, or what used to be shoes, Bas."

Sebastiano threw up his hands.

"Jesus, the shoes again!"

"How'd they get that way?"

"Why's it matter?"

"Hear me out. I've got a plan."

Sebastiano looked down at his shoes. He wiggled his toes through a large hole in one of them. "Dogs, I think. That last night in Huelva before we shipped out."

"Dogs. How did dogs get to your shoes?"

"Not sure, really. I was ... uh ... visiting someone, a friend—"

"You have a friend?"

...

"In Huelva?"

Sebastiano shrugged. "Kind of a new friend, you might say... Okay, temporary friend. Fussy oriental lady. She asked me to leave my shoes outside. And when I came out, bing-bing, they're gone."

"How'd you get them back?"

"Wasn't easy, Melo. Do you realize how painful it is to walk around on cobblestones barefoot? Anyway, I found what was left of one of them in the alley, and then the other one in the street, all slobbered. Somebody must have pinched them and threw them out where the dogs could play with them."

"Eat them, it looks like, and then threw them up."

"Indigestible, I guess."

"Must be awfully hard to work in."

"I get along pretty well."

"Yes," said Carmelo, "you do, like all tough sailors do when they're far away at sea."

"Right."

"But it's so ... un... unprofessional. So, unbecoming."

"Who on this ship cares how 'becoming' I am?"

Carmelo smiled. "Say that again, and slowly."

"Who on this ship—" Carmelo cast his eyes up. "Who? Him?"

"The master of the ship wants his hand-picked crew to look like professionals. Not like bums."

"You think he really notices?"

"I could call it to his attention. They're pretty comical, those 'shoes.' Not...becoming."

"And why would you want me to get in trouble with him, Melo? Why would you call his attention to my shoes?"

"So we could get you some new ones."[94]

73

≈

In Rico's office

"I'LL THINK ABOUT IT," said Rico. "Why should I care about an OB's[05] feet? You're the one who's supposed to be 'able-bodied.'"

"Well, I was thinking, we want wouldn't another accident on this ship, and if Bas isn't in tip-top form, there could be —"

"*Another* accident? Hey! This wasn't my ship when that explosion happened last year.[96] That's how I got this job. They found the other captain negligent and canned his ass."[97]

"Yeah, the Company's not very tolerant of accidents on its ships. Mistakes happen, for sure, but not all of them get reported. Of course, an explosion kind of reports itself..."

"Are you saying that that guy's an accident waiting to happen?"

"Oh, no! No...well, not... not for sure. I'm just thinking about safety. We need to be extra careful when we're in an American port. I just think Bas isn't working up to his usual level, and being hobbled by bad shoes might have something to do with it."

"Bullshit!"

"And ... and besides, he's my *compare*, Captain, and a good friend."

"Like I said, I'll think about it. Sounds like a flimsy excuse to get ashore, that's all."

Carmelo turned to walk out, but stopped, then turned back to the captain.

"Now that you mention 'ashore,' you realize I didn't go out with you guys that last night in Huelva. I stayed with the skeleton crew and watched the ship while you guys—while you guys 'recreated.'"

"And your point?" asked Rico.

"I'm just saying, it's been a long time, Captain. I myself could use a little shore leave. Know what I mean? Not even a whole night. Maybe only an afternoon? You know, to walk around on land a bit, to 'recreate?'"

Rico blinked. Twice. Then roared with laughter. He slammed his palm onto his forehead.

"Hahaha! Petty sneaky, Melo. 'Oh, Captain, my poor *compare* needs some new shoes. I could go ashore with him and help him slip into something more...more 'comfortable!' Hahaha! You're such a terrible liar, little Melo."

Carmelo squirmed, then threw up his hands. "I...was just...try—"

"*Basta*! Talk to me again when we get to Baltimore. I've got a lot of paperwork to do before then."

10 ⋈ Child of Mary

❖ *I, Nellie Rose Cascio, a member of the Sodality of the Children of Mary, promise to love, honor, worship, and consecrate my life to the most Holy and Blessed Trinity, the Father, the Son, and the Holy Spirit.*

❖ *I promise to love our Blessed Mother, to pray the Rosary every day, and to wear the scapular.*

❖ *I promise to encourage unity of our family by praying the Rosary together every day and to remind them that the family that prays together, stays together.*

❖ *I promise to attend Holy Mass every Sunday and spend as much time as possible in adoration of the Holy Eucharist.*

❖ *I promise to be a good and obedient child, to keep myself pure and innocent, and to avoid the occasions of sin.*

❖ *I promise to love Jesus with all my heart, to love our Blessed Mother, and to love and honor Saint Joseph.*

❖ *I promise to receive the Holy Eucharist as often as I can and to attend Mass on the First Sunday of each month with the Sodality of the Children of Mary.*

NELLIE, AT FIFTEEN, vowed to practice saying that pledge over and over every day for the whole six months' waiting period.[98] She wanted her recitation to be absolutely perfect, with not even the tiniest mistake or hesitation, at the induction ceremony of the Children of Mary Sodality in August. She wanted to join that

Sodality almost as much as she wanted to become a nun. For her, it was a kind of preparatory phase before applying for the novitiate, a kind of self-conducted basic training.

The sisterhood of the Sodality became the harbor for Nellie's highest spiritual aspirations. While many Catholic young girls and women welcomed Sodality membership as a base for socializing, some, like Nellie and her close friend, Fran Macaluso, immersed themselves in its sacred nature as a confraternity in the Catholic Church. In addition to the religious and moral practices to which they swore perpetual allegiance, the group also performed many acts of benevolent and religious service. Though she worked in the fields or in the knitting mill most days, she spent almost all of whatever time she had left engaged in what a wag had once called "celestial housekeeping."[99] She loved even the most menial tasks if they involved the Church or a religious event. Cleaning the altar, polishing candlesticks, washing the cassocks and surplices of the altar boys, sweeping floors—these were for Nellie and Fran and a few other serious members a form of prayer, an act of consecration to Almighty God, and to their beloved patron, the Blessed Virgin Mary.

However, this form of sisterhood was also a social experience for Nellie. It involved working with the other members to operate the frequent bake sales that raised money for the Church. They cooked for and helped stage many of the feast day celebrations, and worked with other service organizations to provide the Jesus-mandated basic human aid to the needy classified as "corporal works of mercy."[100]

Showtime

BETWEEN FULL-TIME WORK and her Sodality, Nellie's was a full, if not a fully satisfying, life. Work helped sustain her family, and the Sodality sustained her spirit. But she was a teenager and needed a bit of fun in her life, too. In Mount Morris, New York in the mid-1920s there weren't many fun options for a young woman, especially one who had ardently dedicated herself "to be a good and obedient child, to keep myself pure and innocent, and to avoid the occasions of sin."

The rising movie industry provided Nellie with what she needed. It captured the imaginations of even religiously-committed teen girls. Watching everything from the quaint antics of Charlie Chaplin to the breathtaking sweeps of DeMille's epics, Nellie spent some time—and a nickel of her pay[101]—almost every weekend at the Family Theater.

Shortchanged

"**WHERE'S THE REST** of the money?" asked Mike Cascio as he peered deeper into the pay envelope. "There's less than usual."

Nellie blushed. "Papa, I...I was...I was sick on Tuesday and couldn't go in."

"You seem all right now."

"Yes. Mama helped me before she left for work. She was a little late that day and probably got docked for it, too. Sorry."

Mike brusquely scooped up the money on the table and put it into his pocket. He turned to go. Nellie held out her hand.

"Papa? "What?"

"Can I have my nickel?"

Mike patted his pocket. "That comes out of a full week's pay. You were short this week. No nickel."

He went into the bathroom and closed the door.

Later, Nellie told Fran she wouldn't be going to the movies with her that weekend. Together they saw at least one movie a week, unless there was a church event.

Fran put her arm around Nellie. "I'm not going without you, Natala dearie. We'll do something else. We can go window shopping— try on some hats! Or walk in the park. You can come to my house and we can listen to our new radio."

"Oh? What's on?" asked Nellie.

"Nothing. Farm reports. News." Nellie raised an eyebrow.

"Fine. We'll make cookies."

Nellie said sadly, "No. You should go. It's a Charlie Chaplin and you love him."

"Not as much as I love you, sweetie. And besides, it's a nickel I can put away to see *Ben Hur* this Christmas. That'll cost more than these little comedies because it's DeMille and in color.

"Oh, yes, yes," replied Nellie. "Wouldn't want to miss that. They're calling it *A Tale of the Christ*. It was on the poster. I love religious movies. *King of Kings* was like being in church!"

Now it was Fran's turn to raise an eyebrow. "Hmmm. Your eyes were closed in prayer during Mary Magdalene's hoochie-coochie?"[102]

Nellie threw her a stern look. "She hadn't converted to Jesus yet, Fran! She was lost in sin. Saving people from sin is what the Christ does."

Fran looked intently into Nellie's eyes and smiled broadly. "You're so ... dedicated, Nellie. I love that about you! So devoted. I never thought of a movie theater as a church."

"Not all the time, Fran. Charlie Chaplin, Buster Keaton, and even Fatty Arbuckle[103] crack me up. But seeing religious things on a big movie screen, draws me all in. It's very real to me."

"Me, too, but maybe not as much as you, Nellie. You're a real Child of Mary and I know you're going to be accepted into the Sodality."

Nellie pointed at Fran. "You will be, too. I'm praying for you."

"Thanks, Natala."

She extended her hand.

Nellie took it limply.

"It's a deal," Fran said, "Cheer up! We'll goof off outside the theater, while that little tramp goofs off inside."

11 ◁ Shore Leaving

"Exit"

THE *FALERIA* HAD BEEN SNUGGED into her berth at Baltimore's Curtis Bay and operations had begun to unload its cargo of manganese ore for the Davison Chemical Company. The crew was scrambling to open cargo holds and make other preparations for the transfer. Ship maintenance was also begun, some tasks best done in port. But some best, and usually, done at sea.[104]

Rico knelt to peer into one of his ship's fuel tanks. He quickly drew back as he caught a whiff of fumes. He spun on his knees and stood up.

"Tonight!" he called out to the crew. "Get this thing cleaned out so we can fuel up and go."

He stood and glanced at his watch.

"Start at sunset and work fast. I want the sludge to disperse by morning. In the meantime, get the pressure steamers set up, get the hoses connected, put the discharge lines in place—the whole thing—you know the drill. Just pretend you're at sea."

The men scattered to their various stations to start the complex process of flushing the tank. Carmelo approached Rico, as Sebastiano hung back and tried to look busy with coils of rope.

"Looks like everybody's on the job, Captain. This might be a good time for that ... shopping trip we talked about a few days ago. That shoe situation has gotten worse. They should be replaced before we set out again."

Rico looked over at Sebastiano, who scuttled around behind the ropes to hide his feet.

"Ah, yes, time for a foot job—I mean, new shoes for the poor *marinaio*. Sorry, I don't think so, Melo. I need you guys here to be sure we're ready to do the deed and zip out."

"But we're all caught up and it's several hours until sunset. I only asked for a quick...just an afternoon. We'll be quick, Captain!"

"Ah, yes, Tosto will be *tosto!*" roared Rico. He sniffed. "And my poor *compare* can get himself a quick pair of shoes in the meantime. I don't know, Melo. What if you guys get mugged?"

Carmelo waved to Sebastiano to come join them. "Look at this guy," he said. "Nobody's going to mess with me while he's in my shadow."

Sebastiano bared his teeth.

Carmelo pleaded, "Please, Captain. It's another week until Tampa, and I remind you, I stayed on board while you and the guys—"

"Ah, Huelva! What a night! You're a persistent little ball-breaker, you know."

"Is there something I can bring back for you, some cigars maybe?"

"Don't need cigars. Got the finest Cubans already."

"Okay. Anything else?"

Rico grinned. "What I want, nobody can drag onto this ship, *compare*. I can wait for Tampa."

"And you can spare us for a few quick hours, Captain. You know you can. Man to man, give me a—"

"You know," said Rico. "I've heard about those *Americano* cowboy cigars. Maybe you can pick me up some—if you don't spend all night looking! 'Stogas,' I think they're called."

"Stogas? Okay, I'll ask around for some Stogas. Cowboy cigars."

Carmelo turned to go. Then turned back. "Thanks, Rico, it means a lot to me, you know—man to man." He winked.

Rico fished in his pocket for some lire.

"Yeah, yeah. You'll need money. Get these changed for dollars. And if you have any left over from the...the shoes—ha-ha—get me some cigars."

12 ⋈ Shortcomings

THE CHILDREN OF MARY, many of whom were adult women, served the food while the wedding guests reveled. It was an appropriate act of Sodality service since marriage was a sacrament and thus worthy of celebration. As the sacred fount from which issued the next generations, a wedding was the transition arena where girls began to fulfill their destinies as mothers, in emulation of their patron, Mary, the Blessed Virgin, who was also the Mother of God.

Nellie Cascio believed this Mariology[105] with all her heart. And believed every wrinkle of the lore that unfolded from it: from the Nativity to the Crucifixion; from the pantheon of the saints to the celebrations of their feast days; from the official personages and structures of the Catholic Church to the patriarchy that rigidly constrained her daily life. When she felt the stirrings of resentment against some of its constraints, those feelings were quickly squelched by the overriding assumption that she, like all people, was an essentially flawed and sinful victim of the Devil's legendary rebellion against the Creator, as told in the Bible.

Moreover, as a descendant of Eve, the first woman, she had to contend with the inherent weakness and impiousness inherited from that original sinner. She took her role as a Child of Mary so seriously that she eschewed the common preoccupations and dalliances of young women of her time: dating and dreaming of a married future. In her deepest well of desire, she longed to circumvent the fate of all those brides at whose weddings she served, and ascend to the only other role a woman could respectably attain by becoming a Catholic nun living a contemplative life in a cloistered monastery. As a nun, she could serve God directly, consecrate her body and soul to the holy work of the Church, and avoid the pain, disappointment, and sadness that made up the more likely fate of a married woman. It's what she saw in her own family, with a mother who had only hard manual labor in the fields to look forward to between bouts of pregnancy and birthing.

She was glad she was not alone in this aspiration. Her good friend, Fran Macaluso, shared it. The Sisters who taught at the Catholic primary school in Mount Morris lived in a convent nearby. Nellie and Fran pondered on how to arrange an interview there.

"Why don't we just go ask one of the Sisters at St. Patrick's?" asked Fran.

Nellie threw up her hands and shook her head. "Oh, no, no, that's the kind of thing teachers talk to parents about! If my papa found out he'd get so mad! And he'd probably clamp down even more on what I can do. It's bad enough now, Fran."

"Right," said Fran. "Why can't some parents see what a blessing it is to have a nun in the family?"

"They'd rather have a wage earner in the family these days."

Fran pointed to one of her legs. "Mine might appreciate having someone else take care of their crippled kid."[106]

"Stop with that!" said Nellie. "You're not crippled. One leg's a

84

little shorter than the other. You get around fine."

"Not everybody thinks that way, Natala. It doesn't look good, the limping."

"God doesn't notice it when you're praying, doing good works, serving Him. It's what's in your heart, Frannie, not your leg."

The two thought quietly for several moments.

"Well, I could go and ask," said Fran. "My family wouldn't care if the nuns told on me. Let's go over. I'll ask to speak to a Sister and find out what a girl needs to do to become a nun. You can wait outside."

"That might work. But don't mention me. Don't say something like 'me and my friend are interested in becoming nuns.' Just say you're the one, and that I'm...I'm there to walk you home."

"Helping the handicapped," said Fran with a wry smile. Nellie poked her. They laughed.

At the convent

THE NEXT WEEK, as she waited for Fran on a step outside the convent, Nellie prayed for her friend. She asked God to give her eloquence to say convincing words, and the inspiration to ask the right questions, and for the capacity to get and retain the information she'd need to apply for admission to become a nun. Nellie knew if she were accepted, it would take years before she would become a true nun, but she was willing to put in the time, filling it with prayer and good works. The big hurdle would be getting the convent to accept her without her parents' permission. Gloom settled on her as she realized how tall a hurdle it was.

Too soon, the door opened, and Fran limped out. The door clicked closed and Fran stood there in tears.

"What's wrong, Frannie?" asked Nellie as she rushed up to her.

Fran said nothing for a long time. Finally, she composed herself and took Nellie by the arm.

"Let's just go now."

They walked slowly back toward home.

"Well, whatever it was," said Nellie, "it doesn't look like good news. Tell me!"

Fran stopped. "They don't take cripples," she said almost in a whisper.

"What?"

"Maybe some convents will take cripples but this one doesn't. Not for becoming a nun. Thank you very much. Goodbye, kid."

"But...but that...that doesn't sound...." Nellie looked back at the convent. "That's not Christian, that's not right! There must be some other—"

"It's a burden on them. Like on my parents. They only want able-bodied—"

"Ridiculous! You're a good person, Frannie. You can do the work, you can pray, you can do whatever—"

"Apparently not," replied Fran. "They'd take you. Why don't you go and apply?"

"You know why. I was hoping to find out if I could get in without having my papa's permission. But now...now I'm not so sure if I even want to apply. If they won't take my sweet, beautiful friend, then there's something wrong with them."

"Well, frankly, it came as a surprise to me. The sister only let me talk for a few minutes. Then she went out and brought another sister in. They asked me to stand and walk across the room. That's when they said they couldn't take...somebody like me."

She began to cry. Nellie hugged her and stroked her hair.

"Their loss, Frannie. Their loss. We'll just keep looking for the right place and the right time."

"You're such a hopeful person, Nellie. You never give up. I know I can always count on you. And that's only one reason why I love you. Such a true, true friend!"

Trap door

BUT WHAT HER "TRUE FRIEND" didn't tell her was that a trap door had suddenly sprung open beneath Nellie's long-cherished aspirations about the sisterhood, and they plunged into oblivion. It came as a surprise, this sudden loss of hope. Maybe in some future world, religious orders would be more open to admitting applicants with handicaps, but today's snubbing of her dear friend stirred an unexpectedly deep revulsion for any organization with such prejudices. It was another obstructing wall, higher than the one posed by her father's refusal to permit following through on what she thought was her vocation.

And to make it even worse, another wall now loomed even higher. She could not bring herself to break Fran's heart. If she applied for and received admission to the novitiate, it would add to the humiliation of today, even though Fran would never say so. Nellie was not willing to do that. Instead, she would pursue a more personal spiritual life not only within the Sodality and similar lay organizations, but also in a new religious order, established solely within her heart. In this exclusive, private cloister she would safely commune with God and the saints.

Suitors

LIFE IN A VILLAGE like Mount Morris—at the time, not much more than a hamlet—is slow-moving. Once routines are established, life can carry a villager along like a leaf floating on a deep, lazy river. Time slips by hardly noticed. To a young woman with dependencies on her family, deep involvement with Church, and little contact with the wider world that more affluence and education can bring, even the normal awakenings of maturity can meld quietly into the background. To Nellie Cascio, they were on the order of annoyances at best, and threats to her sense of spirituality at worst.

Men, only a scant few of them, would drift into her life, but she regarded them much like a pebble that slips into a shoe. The subject of marriage came up frequently, especially once her sister, Frances—at the age of twenty-three—married a young man from the neighborhood. "Charlie's such a great catch," said one of her friends. "He's so handsome!"

Nellie had replied, "I'm happy for her, but that's not for me. I'm pretty happy with my life the way it is."

"Happy" was the wrong word. She had grown used to her life, satisfied with her sodality work, her jobs at the canning factory and in the knitting mills nearby, and even with the prospect of taking care of her aging parents for the rest of her life. She had come to terms with that. She had learned that aspirations to "better" things could disappoint in the end.

That didn't stop the occasional man from taking an interest in her.[107] Most of them she found frightening and repellent. The butcher next door, Tom Cusimano, kept trying to persuade Mike and Josephine to choose his son, Joey, for Nellie. But her parents were leery of Tom, not only because his butcher shop business wasn't prospering, but also because he had a reputation for throwing knives at people when he got angry.

A milder man from Cuylerville, Leonard Celentano, was suggested. He was a foreman at the canning factory and could have probably supported Nellie and a family as he progressed in the company. Nellie was interested enough in Leonard to spend some time with him, but she abruptly shut down the relationship when he revealed he was secretly an atheist. Nellie wanted a life where she could freely practice her spirituality, stay involved with the Church, and bring up her kids as good Catholics.

There were a few others, usually funneled to the Cascios by members of the Sicilian community in that part of New York State, but most of the men ended the relationship themselves after noting Nellie's religiosity and prudishness.

This tiresome process went on for a few years until the day

Richard Tate[108] came on the scene. Nellie found herself attracted to him despite her usual antipathies toward eligible men. She liked him for several reasons. First, he was tall, unlike most of the men who'd approached her. Also, intriguing, because he wasn't Italian. He was Irish. Tate worked on his family's farm close outside of Rochester. He had gone to business school for a year. He was well-spoken, polite, and much more "American" than most of the men she knew. Oh, and he drove his family's Model A for occasional visits with relatives in nearby Piffard. Probably best of all, he was a devout Catholic, someone she recalled seeing at some church services and gatherings in the past few years.

She confided to Fran, "If I have to get married—and everybody's pushing me to do it—he could be a good match. You know who I mean? Tate? Richard? What do you think?"

Fran stared off into the sky as they walked back from a movie. "Yes, I know him. Tall? Not Italian-looking? Ford car?"

"Yes! Yes, that's him," said Nellie. "Kind of interesting, don't you think?"

Fran fell silent. They walked a little farther.

"What are you thinking, Fran?" asked Nellie. "Come on, tell me!" Fran pointed to a bench up ahead.

"Let's just sit here a second. And talk."

They sat.

"How many times have you seen him?" she asked.

"Just a couple. Why?"

"Just wondering."

"About what?"

"Did you...? I mean, did it get...? Oh, you know what I mean!"

"No. What?"

"Physical."

"What do you mean, 'physical'?"

"Did you ... uh—"

"Get romantic?"

89

"Or ... "

"No, no, of course not! We were in the living room at home."

"Did you hold hands? Did you hug?"

"No. We just talked."

"Skip it. He's a nice guy. Really nice guy. Not that I know much about him—you've obviously spent more time with him than I have. And you like him. That's good, Natala."

"I haven't spent all that much time with him, but yes, he's the most interesting man I've met, Frannie."

Fran stood up.

"Well, I'm so glad to hear that. Especially if he's a strong supporter of the Church and of your religious interests."

"Oh, he is, he really is. We talked about the novenas he makes, his altar boy days—he even speaks Latin from the Mass! He says he's got a special set of holy cards about the Blessed Mother."

"Really?"

"Uh-huh. And his parents are devout, too. And he's going to run the farm sometime in the future, so he'll be an excellent provider."

"Good."

"But I hear you, Fran. It's a serious subject and I don't want to get all fluttery and girlish about it. Marriage is a holy sacrament, blessed by Jesus himself. And Richard sees it that way, too. And, and I'm not a girl anymore. I can think for myself."

Fran hugged her.

"I'm sure you're praying about it, Natala. Pray harder than ever. It's a life-long commitment. And very important."

"I will, Fran. You know that."

She studied Fran's face.

"But I still think there's something you're not telling me. What is it?"

"No, just what I said, sweetie. Also to be very, very thoughtful about making that commitment. And kind. You've waited a long time so far. It won't kill you to wait a bit longer until you're absolutely sure he's the right man for you."

Nellie raised an eyebrow. "All right. Still ..."

≈

Full disclosure

MIKE STUDIED THE VISITOR carefully, scanning his lanky frame from top to bottom. He didn't return Richard's smile. Nellie sat quietly in a corner of the kitchen trying to smile back at Richard. She knew Mike wasn't examining a possible future husband for her, but, assessing the economic impact of having him as a future son-in-law.

"What kind of farmer?" he asked.

"Mostly potatoes, but sometimes we also grow onions and lettuce."

"Rochester? Big city. They got farms in the city?"

Richard drew a broad circle in the air. "Well, you know, the Rochester area, sir, just outside the city to the west. There's a little village nearby called Greece. We farm near there."

Mike looked to Nellie. "Huh?" Nellie translated.

"You are Greek?" asked Mike.

Richard glanced expectantly at Nellie. "Tell him we're Irish. The name of the village nearby is Greece. I don't know why it's called Greece, but we're not Greek."

Nellie said, "*Lui non è greco. Lui è irlandese. La città si chiamava Grecia.*"

Mike seemed satisfied with that. He turned to leave the room. Richard stepped forward and held out a small package.

"I hear you like Stogies. I brought you a couple of packs."

Mike studied the packets, smiled a little and took them. "Yeah, I like," he said and left.

Nellie whooshed in relief. Richard sat and tried to relax.

"He doesn't understand much English," she said. "Just enough to get by on the job. I hope he didn't hurt your feelings."

"Oh, no! Not at all! Well, maybe a little. It's a different kind of ... style. But I'm sure he's a nice man. Do you think he likes me?"

Nellie shrugged. "Hard to tell with him. He's really nice on the inside but he thinks he's got to show he's the boss in this family. Makes him kind of gruff."

"I can handle that. Does it matter if I'm not Italian?"

"Well, it's what a person is used to, I guess. All along this street are Italians, and a lot of them—and I mean a *lot*—are relatives in some way. It doesn't matter to me."

Richard sighed. "Good!"

"What matters to me," said Nellie, "is that you're a religious man, a Catholic. I get nervous around non-Catholics. Especially atheists!"

"And that's what I appreciate about you, Nellie. You're a devoted Catholic, active in your Church, and high-minded in everything."

Nellie rose. "Can I get you something to drink, some lemonade, water, or wine, or ... "

"Oh, some water would be nice, Nellie."

"Fine! Why don't you take off your jacket? You must be warm in that thing."

She went to the icebox. Richard removed his jacket, then quickly put it back on. When Nellie returned, she laughed and said, "The water's cool, Richard, but I'm sure you'd be more comfortable without that jacket."

"Wouldn't your parents think it's too informal for me to be in shirtsleeves? "

Nellie set the drinks down and went over to him. "No, it's all right. Here, let me help you—"

"Oh! If ... if you ... think it's—"

Nellie draped the coat over a chair back. Richard stood with his arms folded. Nellie handed him a glass of water, which he took with his right hand, but immediately he put his left hand into his pants pocket.

"Have a seat, relax. You look uncomfortable. Is there something wrong?"

Richard sat with his left hand in his pocket. His face flushed. He took a long sip of the water. Nellie studied him and a cloud of concern came over her face.

"What is it, Richard? This is very strange."

He put down the glass and looked steadily into her eyes.

"Nellie, there's something you should know. I ... I was going to tell you ... later, after we got to know each other a little better. But I think our friendship is moving a lot faster than I expected!"

Nellie sat and took his hand.

"It's going fine, Richard. We have so much in common. It's interesting talking to you. You can tell me anything—Wait! You're not a secret atheist, are you? No, I don't think you would be. What is it?"

Richard withdrew his left hand from his pocket and laid his arm on the table. With both arms side-by-side, no hand projected beyond the cuff of the left shirtsleeve.

Nellie gasped.

"Oh! I mean ... oh! Your arm, it's ... "

"I was born this way. I'm usually not bothered by it —"

"*Born* that way?"

"Yes. I've adjusted pretty well. Just didn't want t–"

"I didn't realize ... " murmured Nellie.

"It doesn't keep me from doing the accounting for the farm. Like I said, I've adjusted. I didn't want it to come up so soon after we met. And don't look at me that way, I hate sympathy! I know I couldn't keep it from you forever but I thought we could get to know each other a little better first."

"Oh," said Nellie flatly.

She looked away from him, drawn into a vision of Fran limping away from the convent, a shadowy nun figure closing the door with a click, cruelly shutting out her dear friend. And shattering Nellie's lifelong dream.

"Does it bother you?" said Richard, breaking the spell.

With a start, Nellie said, "No! No, I'm sorry ... for you, I mean."

"I said, sympathy is not— "

"It is a surprise, though. Excuse me for getting a little flustered. I didn't mean to ... "

Richard stood and put on his coat.

"I should go now. You're upset, I can see that. I'll let you think about it on your own for a while. Let me know when we can meet again—that is, if you think we can meet again."[109]

He went to the door.

"Oh, Richard, I'm so sorry for this. It's a personal thing, nothing to do with you. You're a good man, a really fine man, I know that. And I haven't seen any men—aside from priests—who are as good as you. I'll explain my problem to you. But later, after I get better control of myself."

She tiptoed to peck him on the cheek. "Thank you for coming today. And thank you for bringing my papa the cigars."

Richard touched his cheek with his right hand.

"Goodbye, Nellie."

13 ⋈ Busted

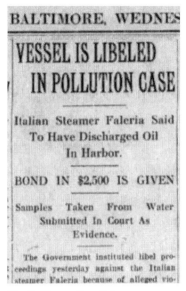

BALTIMORE, WEDNES

VESSEL IS LIBELED IN POLLUTION CASE

Italian Steamer Faleria Said To Have Discharged Oil In Harbor.

BOND IN $2,500 IS GIVEN

Samples Taken From Water Submitted In Court As Evidence.

The Government instituted libel proceedings yesterday against the Italian steamer Faleria because of alleged vio-

The Baltimore Sun, July 29, 1925

RICO WAS DEFIANT. George W. Collier, United States Marshal, flanked by two security guards, had come aboard and served him documents instituting legal proceedings against the owners of the *Faleria*.

"It wasn't that much!" he boomed. "Accidents happen, and we cleaned it up right away."

Marshal Collier, shook his head. "It wasn't an accident, Captain. And you didn't start to clean it up until we cited you."

Rico shrugged.

Collier pressed on, "Even if it was a little oil—which it definitely wasn't—a little oil in itself isn't the problem. But a little oil from a thousand ships like the *Faleria* that tie up in Baltimore harbor every year—that adds up to a massive pollution problem. Not only is it unpleasant, sir, it's also dangerous. If that oil should catch

95

fire–"

"But $2500 for just one little spill?" bellowed Rico. "That's a good chunk of the profits. Might as well have left that ore in Genoa."

"You might as well have left that sludge on your ship instead of discharging it into our harbor, Captain."

"Shit! This is robbery! *Armed* robbery by the look of your guys. Do the French or the British get dinged that much? Only the Italians and the Germans?"

"I don't know, Captain Mancuso. The new regulations were passed just last year[110] and we don't have much of a record yet. In fact, you're the first violation."

Rico was silent a few moments. "It's political, isn't it? Mussolini, right? *Il Duce* is looking more and more like a warrior, isn't he, a Commander-in-Chief? But hey, Marshal, don't take it out on us. If you haven't noticed, we're *merchant* marines, not *warrior* marines. We're simple sailors, haulers of freight, keeping the economies going. Fining my company isn't going to stop a military buildup in Italy. Come on, give me a break. At least reduce the fine."

"It's not a fine, sir. It's a bond.[111] We need your owners to send a representative to a court hearing next week. He can make a case why the *Faleria* is innocent of the charge of polluting the waters of Baltimore harbor."

"That's not going to happen," said Rico. "The company isn't going to send somebody across the ocean to speak to a goddam court. That's crazy. And besides, I've got cargo to load in Tampa—if they don't fire me for this, this piracy."

"Uh, just trying to be helpful here, sir, but the company could empower you to be their representative. Your English is pretty good. You could make a case why the company shouldn't be fined. Perhaps all they need is a good explan–"

"I told you, a couple of careless deck hands. They're hiding but

I'm going to fire them—and worse—when I catch them. Anyway, nobody's going to show up in your court."

"Well, we'll just have to wait until then and hope for the best, Captain. Just so you know, that's what a bond or a 'lien' is for. It is a guarantee of your appearance. If no one shows, as you predict, then the bond money is forfeited."

"I'm not putting up any goddam $2500!" [112]

George Collier smiled weakly. "$2500 is a lot less than a whole ship, sir. You have three choices: pay the bond and show up at a court hearing, or don't pay the bond and we take your ship – tonight. Or pay the bond, leave the port, and surrender the $2500."

Collier rose to leave. He drew a business card out of his pocket. "We'll need the money by the end of the day. Here's my card, in case you want to talk further. Otherwise, all the details are spelled out in those documents. Good day, sir."

As the group left the room, Rico muttered, "*Vaffanculo,*" and crammed the papers into a desk drawer.

"What?" asked Collier from the doorway.

"Get off my ship now!"

14 ⋈ *Via Piccola Italia*

CARMELO AND SEBASTIANO FLASHED their passes at the gangplank and a few steps later set foot on the pier at Curtis Bay in Baltimore Harbor. They were now in *l'America,* the actual United States of America.

"I can't believe we did it, Melo!"

"Just keep walking normally ... or as normally as you can in those *stronzi* on your feet."

"Hey!" said Sebastiano, "watch what you call turds. These are 'freedom boots.' Show more respect."

"I suppose you're right. Without them, we'd probably be safe and snug in jail now—for tampering with a goddam fuel tank valve. Oh, *mi scusi, mi scusi, Signore 'Freedom Boots.'*"

They wove their way around buildings till they came out on a city street. They surveyed their surroundings.

"Where to now, Melo?"

"I don't know, Bas. Just keep moving farther and farther away from the ship. Get deeper into the city. Look around for people who might be able to help."

"And speak Italian," said Sebastiano.

"Well," said Carmelo, "there's that. Keep your ears open. Gotta be people around a harbor from all countries. Anyway, I hope so."

Sebastiano pointed toward the harbor.

"*Faleria's* over there, so I guess we head off over this way."

He indicated a busy commercial street and they strode toward it. At the corner stood a Baltimore policeman, who eyed them carefully. Seeing him, they crossed to the other side of the street and walked a little faster. The policeman crossed and followed them.

"Maybe we shouldn't look too much like we're in a hurry, running away from him," said Carmelo. "Slow down. Tie your shoe, or what's left of it."

Sebastiano stopped, crouched and fiddled with the shoestrings. The policeman caught up with them.

"Help you, boys?"

They stared at him in silence. "I say, are you lost?"

Carmelo pointed to his mouth.

"*Non parlare inglese,*" he said.

The policeman looked toward the harbor.

"Sounds Italian. Sailors from that Italian ship? *Faleria*, I think? Something's going on there. US Marshal's car been parked there all morning."

At the sound of their ship's name, the sailors brightened.

"*Faleria! Si, Italiano,*" said Sebastiano.

The policeman circled them, taking particular note of Sebastiano's shoes.

"You ain't gonna get far in them things, sailor. What happened?"

Carmelo pointed to the shoes, then to the store fronts. He took out the lire Rico had given him.

"*Scarpe, scarpe,*" he said.

"Money? Ah, you wanna buy shoes for this guy, I get it."

He pointed to the lire and then to a storefront across the street.

"You need to change these and get some dollars. Money change, over there. Make into ... dollar ... *dollaro*?"

The sailors looked across the street. Then at the money in Carmelo's hand.

The policeman, with alternating arm thrusts, said, "Italian money make into Americano money. *Leeray. Dollaray.* Get it?"

Carmelo remembered what Rico had said about changing money as soon as they got off the ship. He smiled at the policeman.

"Ah. Grazie! Mille grazie!"

"Over there."

They started across the street. The policeman held up his hand. "Whoa. Hold on, hold on. I don't know any shoe stores around here. So ask inside the money change." He pointed to Sebastiano's shoes, and then to the money, then to the money change. *"Inglishay,* 'Shoe store.'"

Carmelo repeated, "*Ah, si*. Shoe store. Shoe store."

The policeman nodded and pointed to the money change.

Sebastiano said, "I think he says they got shoes in there. Change money and buy shoes in the same place. Sounds odd, but in America, who knows how they do things."

Carmelo smiled and nodded toward the policeman and turned to cross the street.

"Grazie. Molto grazie, Signore," he said. "Come on, Bas. Let's see what they got in there."

They waved to the policeman.

The store was busy. A small line had formed outside the teller's cage at the back. The sailors got in line.

"I don't see any shoes here," said Sebastiano. "Just cigarettes and candy and trinkets."

"Right," said Carmelo. "Maybe there's another room—" He stopped when he heard the customer at the head of the line say something in Italian.

"Hey, Bas, that guy just said *'ragazze'*. In Italian! Somebody who speaks Italian!"

Sebastiano leaned out of line and peered ahead.

"That guy was asking about women?"

"I thought so. Sounded like it."

"Women's shoes maybe?"

"Ask him when he comes this way."

The line moved ahead, and the man at the front headed toward them. Sebastiano stepped out of line, smiled at the man and asked him in Italian, "Excuse me, *compare*, we don't speak English. We need to find a place to buy—"

The man was a little tipsy. He grabbed Sebastiano by the shoulders and gave a raucous laugh.

"Hey, *paisano!* Alone in the big city with money to spend before your ship departs?"

"Uh, yes, yes, in a way. We need to buy—"

"The *ragazze* here are pretty cheap. Just be sure they're clean."

"Actually, we're here to buy me some shoes." He pointed to his feet.

"Like I said, the girls are cheap enough you can still buy a pair of shoes better than those. *Madonn—!*"

The line moved ahead. Carmelo approached the clerk behind the cage and held out the lire. Sebastiano stayed back with his new Italian friend.

The clerk said, "What can I do for you?"

Carmelo replied, *"Non parlare inglese."*

"Italiano?" asked the clerk.

"Si."

"Cosa posso fare per lei?"

Carmelo's eyes brightened.

"Parli italiano?"

"Solo un po," replied the clerk. He continued in Italian, "Just enough to get by in this job. Do you want to change those lires for dollars?"

"Si," said Carmelo. *Dolaray.*

The clerk counted out about four dollars' worth of American currency.

Carmelo pointed to the merchandise behind him. "Can I buy shoes here?"

"No, this is just a currency exchange."

"What about that stuff? Can I buy cigars here?"

"Oh yes," replied the clerk. "Pick out what you want and I'll deduct the cost from your dollars."

"Do you have Stogas cigars?"

"Hmmmm....never heard of Stogas. How about Stogies?[113] We have Stogies. Over there."

Carmelo grabbed a package and held it up to the clerk, who handed him his dollars. As he turned to leave, he saw Sebastiano and his "friend" gabbing at the other end of the store.

"Did you ask him where we can buy shoes?" asked Carmelo as he approached.

Sebastiano waved him over.

"Say hello to Giuseppe Materasso. Joe, this is Carmelo Tosto."

The two men shook hands.

"Where you from?" asked Carmelo.

"Napoli," replied Joe. "Your pal here says you guys were looking to make a 'purchase.' To buy something."

"He needs shoes," said Carmelo.

"Ain't no shoe stores around here. Ask the cop outside."

The policeman had lingered outside the exchange, perusing the street most of the time, but occasionally checking on the two sailors he had sent inside.

Carmelo told Joe he had already spoken to the cop but that he didn't know where to find a shoe store.

"But maybe he didn't understand us. You know a little *inglese*, right? Can you ask him for us?"

"Let's give it a shot," said Joe.

The three went out to the policeman and Joe spoke for a few

moments. The policeman looked at the two sailors, then laughed.

"Okay, okay, I know where they can get directions, among other things" he said. He called them closer to him and pointed to a building far down the street, a plain, three-story brick structure, with steps leading up to a door.

He spoke to Joe in English. They both tittered.

"You guys go down there a couple blocks to Jackson Street. See that red-brick building on the corner?"

"Che?"

"Mattoni rossi," said Joe as he pointed it out. "Ask there. They can give you a direction."

The sailors squinted toward the building. They nodded. *"Mattoni rossi, si, si."*

"Ask for Edna," advised the policeman. "She can set you straight." Joe burst into laughter at that. The policeman gave him a wink.

"Ask for Edna,"[114] Joe translated

Carmelo repeated the word.

"Is that like the volcano? I grew up near it."

Joe looked puzzled for a moment.

"Edna?" he said. Then, "Oh, you mean Etna, Mount Etna, the volcano in *Sicilia.*"

Carmelo nodded.

"No! No! *ragazzino.* ED-na, not ET-na. Go now. *Va, marinai!*"

Looking like a scene from a Charlie Chaplin movie, the two sailors set off for the redbrick building, Sebastiano hobbling and catching himself now and then, and Carmelo halting as his companion regained his balance. Joe and the policeman watched with amusement.

Eventually, the two young men reached the redbrick building and climbed the half dozen stairs.

"What are we supposed to say?" asked Sebastiano.

"Edna."

"What does Edna mean?"

"I think it's somebody's name. Or it could mean shoe store."

He knocked. They waited. Upstairs, the corner of a curtain pulled back. He knocked again. With a quick *zip* a small porthole on the door opened and a voice said, "What?"

In Italian, Carmelo said, "Excuse me, we were told you could give us directions to a shoe store."

Silence

Sebastiano pointed to his feet.

"*Scarpe.*" He rubbed his index finger up and down against the pad of his thumb, indicating money. "*Scarpe?*" He pointed to his feet again.

The door opened and an older woman appeared. "They're disgusting! What do you want here?"

Sebastiano made the "spend money" gesture again, pointing to his shoes.

"Yeah, they're pretty bad. We can do all kinds of things to your feet, Bud, but what you wear is your business—although I don't think I even want those things in my house. Even the dogs wouldn't want 'em."

Carmelo said, "Edna?"

She looked at him suspiciously.

"Yeah, that's me. Who sent you?" Carmelo repeated the word.

"Wait a sec," she said. She called inside:

"Hey, Concetta, c'mere. Talk Italian to these guys and see what they want." A much younger, and much prettier, woman appeared behind her.

"Sound like Italian sailors. But I don't get what's what with the shoe thing. Talk to 'em."

Carmelo explained they needed to buy his friend new shoes and were told to come here by a cop down the street. The women laughed heartily. Edna looked down the street and said, "That Jake's [115] baiting us again. Cop needs some quota today. Get outta here ya dumb shits." She backed in and slammed the door.

Down on the street again, they discussed their options. Maybe they should turn themselves in to the police. Bad idea, likely to get them sent back to the ship. Try to find someone who speaks Italian? How did that last one work out?

Sebastiano thought a moment then said, "My mother used to say: "*Quando hai perso la strada, prega.* [When you've lost your way, pray.]"

"That something you know how to do?" asked Carmelo. "I have no faith."

"I don't either," replied Sebastiano. "But maybe we should give it a try. The longer we're out here wandering around the more chance somebody's gonna catch us and send us back to the ship."

"You first."

Sebastiano closed his eyes tightly, put his hands together, and tilted his head up. He said, "Hello, God! What the hell do we do now? Save our asses."

He opened his eyes. "Oh, wait, I forgot the most important part." He closed his eyes again. "Please thank you I'm sorry amen."

He opened his eyes. "That's the best I can do. How about you?"

"Can't top that," said Carmelo.

They looked around.

"Nothing," they both said.

Sebastiano said, "Well, it was worth a try. I think that's the way my mother does it. Priest taught her."

"I think you've gotta be a believer, a church person."

Sebastiano snapped his fingers.

"Hey! Hey, what about a priest? Maybe a priest can help."

"Where we gonna find a priest?"

"In a church, Melo!"

Jake sauntered up to them.

"How'd you do, guys?" They stared at him blankly. "Did you find what you wanted in there?" he said, indicating the apartment building.

The sailors shook their heads.

Carmelo said, *"Chiesa? Chiesa cattolica?"*

"What?"

Chiesa!

Sebastiano added, *"Chiesa cattolica."*

"Cattolica? Oh, Cat'lic? You want a Cat'lic church?" He turned to the building. "I guess you know, this ain't one."

Edna banged on the upper window and made a rude gesture at him.

The boys tried not to laugh. Then, looking pleadingly at the policeman, they put their hands in the prayer position.

"Praying? You want to pray?"

"Prega! Prega! Si!"

"Oh, I got it. You want to make a confession. But you didn't even go in—I was watching."

"Chiesa Cattolica?" the men repeated.

"I think ... I think what you boys are looking for is a church? *Chiesa*? Church?"

"Chiesa, si!" they both nodded vigorously in agreement.

"St. Leo's. That's the one you want. A bit of a hike from here, about five miles or so. St. Leo *chiesa cattolica*. Sainta Leo. "

He pointed out another major street and gestured walking with his fingers.

Sebastiano said, *"Chiesa cattolica Santa Leo?"*

"That's right. *Si*. Lots of Italians in that part of Baltimore. They call it Little Italy. Just start walking that way." He made the fingers-walking gesture again. The sailors looked dubious.

"Don't worry. I feel sorry for you chumps. Go that way. Ask for St. Leo's. Say it: 'Saint Leo's.'"

"Santa Leo's."[116]

"Good enough. Okay, get on your way then. St. Leo's. Priests. Confession. Italians. Go!"

In Fr. Ognibene's office

HIS NON-ITALIAN PARISHIONERS tended to pronounce his last name *Og-na-bean*, but he never corrected them. It kept him humble and reminded him of how far he was from expressing the real meaning of his name: *all good* or Ognibene.[117] Fr. Clint Ognibene didn't like it that his parents had named him Clint. His father said it was because he'd heard the name in a western movie and thought it would help his son fit in better as he grew up. It was more *Americano*. Many of the parishioners simply called him Father O.

Maria Clara, his assistant for the past thirty years, knocked at the door of his office.

"Come in," he called.

Maria Clara was a beautiful woman long past her prime.

"I got a couple of Italian sailors outside and they want to talk to a priest. In Italian."

"Do you know what they want to talk about?"

"Something about shoes. One of them is pretty beat up."

"He needs a doctor?"

"No, it's his shoes—total wrecks. I guess they're begging for shoes. You'd better talk with them."

"Okay, I'll go take a look."

On the church steps, Carmelo and Sebastiano sat and rested after their long walk. Ognibene came out.

"Hello, gentlemen."

The men turned and waved. "How can I help you?" he asked.

"Parli l'italiano?" asked Carmelo.

The priest sat on the steps next to them. He began speaking to them in Italian.

"What can we do for you?"

Carmelo told him how they had come off a ship in harbor and had intended to buy some new shoes for Sebastiano, but had had a difficult time because they didn't speak English and got lost and a policeman had directed them to this church and ... well, that wasn't the whole story but they were glad to be here where they could communicate more easily.

Ognibene asked, "You want to buy shoes? Okay, I can show you where to do that. But first, it looks like you guys could use some rest. Maybe something to drink?"

They nodded.

The priest turned to the door where Maria Clara was discreetly waiting.

"Bring our guests here some water, please, Clare."

"Okay."

"No, let's go inside to my office and we can talk, okay?"

He led them into the church and to his office.

"What are your names?"

"Carmelo."

"Sebastiano."

"I am Fr. Ognibene. 'Father O' to many here. Take off your ... shoes, Sebastiano. Rest your feet. Do they hurt?"

Sebastiano nodded.

"What happened to your shoes?"

"Dogs," said Sebastiano.

As he started to give details Carmelo broke in.

"You ... you don't wanna know, Father."

Maria Clara brought in a tray. There was water, and a couple of sandwiches.

"Ah!" said Fr. O. "You read my mind, Clare. These boys look hungry as well as tired."

"That's plain to see," said Clara. She turned and left.

The sailors inhaled the sandwiches and drew long drafts of the water.

"How long are you in port?"

Carmelo cleared his throat.

"Well," he said. "That's another thing we'd like to talk to you about."

Sebastiano added, "The ship leaves tomorrow, probably. But we don't want to be on it.

"Why not?"

The sailors looked at each other.

Sebastiano said, "You explain, Melo."

Carmelo told about Mussolini and the probable conscription of merchant marine sailors for military service. And that they were hoping to escape to America and get connected to Sebastiano's family who lived in New York.

"So, you're escapees from a dictator?"

They nodded.

"More like refugees, it seems to me," said Ognibene.

"It's all right? America takes 'refugees'?"

"Of course! I can't imagine why America would ever refuse refuge to people who are fleeing from oppression."

"*Grazie, l'A*merica," said Carmelo.

"My uncle loves it here," said Sebastiano. "He lives in *Bruculinu* —know where that is? We would like to go there and see if he will take us in, get us some jobs."

The priest took out a booklet from a desk drawer and thumbed through the pages.

"There's something new called Catholic Charities that just got started here in Baltimore a couple years ago.[118] I can put you in touch with them and they'll be able to help. They can get you a place to sleep, some civilian clothes—including better shoes, Sebastiano!—and help you make contact with your uncle."

The sailors smiled broadly. Sebastiano punched Carmelo on the shoulder.

"See! I told you, Melo. 'When you lose your way, pray!' It goddam works! Uh—I mean God … does good work."

Ognibene asked, "You prayed?"

Sebastiano nodded vigorously.

"Well, I like that," said Ognibene. "Brought you here anyway."

Carmelo added, "The policeman ... "

"God works in ways that aren't always obvious."

"Yes indeed," said Sebastiano. "We're here. *l'America*!"

Carmelo smiled. "From floating *l'italia* to *Piccola Italia* in *l'America. Grazie*, Father. You have saved our lives."

15 ⋈ Bruculinu and Beyond

The Brooklyn Bridge, 1920s

The Little Italians

OVER THE NEXT FEW WEEKS, the essence of the sea began evaporating from Carmelo and Sebastiano. There was soil beneath their feet as they explored the section of Baltimore named "Little Italy" while awaiting word from Catholic Charities. They had gone from a rigidly circumscribed floating village to the vast, variegated, and often confusing carnival that was this new land. They struggled to find words to express their astonishment, especially in English. But with time, assistance, and persistence, they acquired the use of a few English words so people nearby might understand them bettr. And when English failed them, they were likely to encounter someone who understood their native tongue—even their distinctive east Sicilian dialect.

It was hard to ignore the musicality of the Italian language that swirled all around them. Seasoned with diverse regional variations from the Old Country, it mixed with the lower-class American English that constituted its base to generate its own *patois*, or mixture of the two main languages. The new *patois* was neither Italian nor English, but was surprisingly practical—most English speakers could understand them. It included such words as *baccowsa* for outhouse, *giobba* for job, *bosso* for boss, *ticchetto* for ticket, *trocco* for truck, *sciabola* for shovel. It made sense if you listened "loosely": *tu sei un guda boia; gud morni; olraiti; sciusi; bred; iessi*. Sebastiano's uncle, Tony, lived in *Bruculinu*.

The sailors were given civilian clothes, haircuts, and a tiny English-Italian dictionary, which neither of them could use because neither could read in any language. They were lodged in a shelter while social workers searched for ways to get them safely infused into the network of Italians that would deliver them to Sebastiano's uncle in *Bruculinu*. His uncle's name was Tony D'Urso.[119] Through word-of-mouth and a series of letter exchanges with the dozens of people with D'Urso surnames, they located Tony. He worked in the Fulton Fish Market[120] near the Brooklyn Bridge along the East River waterfront in Lower Manhattan.

"He's a Riposto *paisano*,"[121] said Sebastiano. "Works with fish since a kid."

"My hometown," agreed Carmelo. "I can do that work, too. Both can."

The case worker, Grace Timpano,[122] spoke to them in Italian.

"Well, first, we've got to establish contact with him and give him the information about you, Mr. Grasso. I'll send your uncle more detail than in our initial inquiry letter. We'd also like to know if he can help defray some of the cost of sending you to Brooklyn—if he's willing to take you in."

The boys were excited at the prospect of having *compari* in America, even actual *family*.

Carmelo nodded enthusiastically at Grace. "Thank you, thank you for doing this. We feel safe here."

She smiled back. "It's what Catholic Charities is dedicated to, Mr. Tosto. You are safe here, and I think we'll have you placed even more securely soon, very soon."

As they walked back to the shelter, Sebastiano could contain himself no longer. "Melo! We're in a dream! It's like in heaven. Hard to believe. I'm so happy here in America."

Carmelo had to agree. There had been no precedents for this degree of freedom and opportunity in their experience. He had always thought the reports from those who wrote back from America to their Italian relatives were exaggerated. He hadn't seen any golden streets yet, but almost everything else he saw flashed like a heavenly vision.

They walked on for a few more minutes.

"The lady was nice," said Sebastiano.

"Who?"

"The Catholic Charities lady. Nice woman. Grace. Good looking."

"Hmmmm...," said Carmelo. "Yes. Nice lady."

Suddenly he grabbed Sebastiano.

"Hey! Don't get any ideas, Bas. Last thing we need is to piss off someone who's trying to help us."

"I wasn't thinking of anything. Just that she's like America. Friendly, helpful ... ."

"And 'good looking,' you said."

"And too old for me. I wonder if she has a younger sister, or a cousin ... Anyway, things look pretty good here, don't they, Melo! Nice buildings, nice streets, stores, people smile a lot more. She's like America."

"Cool down, Bas. We're still too close to the harbor for my comfort. A wrong move and we could get deported."

"Yes, right. I know. We've gotta behave."

"You especially!"

They shoved each other and continued on with a step lighter than ever on a ship. They were on dry ground. Solid ground. They were eager to pick up a *sciabola* and dig in.

≈

Some days later at the Catholic Charities office

GRACE TIMPANO handed them envelopes.

"Inside these are train tickets, a map, a letter of introduction, a couple of dollars, and instructions in Italian on what to do. These will take you to New York City. To Penn Station."

She handed them cardboard signs about the size of a sheet of paper, with the word "D'Urso" printed on them.

"When you get there, hold these up. We've contacted your uncle, Sebastiano, and he will be waiting at the train station. He'll be looking at the crowd for these signs. *Capite*?"

Carmelo and Sebastiano took the signs and held them in front of their chests.

"How about put 'Riposto' on the sign?" said Carmelo.

Grace took the signs back. "Okay," she said as she began to print the word below their names. In English she muttered, "This should narrow down the field."

"Lots of D'Urso in Riposto," said Sebastiano. Grace gave him a skeptical look.

"And they all show up at Penn Station at 4:17 pm on Thursday. Right."

"Just kidding. You got a younger sister?"

Grace put down her marker.

"What?"

"Nothing."

"Why do you want to know?"

Sebastiano squirmed as Carmelo rolled his eyes.

"Sorry, just thinking, you've been so nice to us, I was wondering... "

"Oh," said Grace. "Thanks, but that's private information. We don't share—"

"Right. Yes, I understand. *Mi scusi.*"

She smiled wryly and went back to printing on the cards. "*Cretino,*" whispered Carmelo.

She finished the printing and handed the cards back to them. "At worst, you could meet a *paisano,*" she said.

"Maybe."

She stood and moved toward the doorway.

"Keep these in the valises we gave you with your things. Someone will come to your shelter tomorrow and drive you to the train station. Any questions?"

Sebastiano started to speak but Carmelo stopped him.

"No, not now," he said. "Thank you for all your help. And excuse my friend here." He jabbed Sebastiano with a thumb.

Grace laughed. "Oh, it's all right.. Glad we could help."

The men turned to leave.

"And, yes, I do have a cousin, Mr. Grasso. But she lives far from here. In the middle of New York State, in fact. Goodbye, boys."

At Home with Uncle Tony

NEW YORK CITY was a big place. In 1925, the Pennsylvania Station took up a couple of square blocks in the midtown area. For a long time no one approached Carmelo and Sebastiano wearing their "D'Urso/Riposto" signs.

Until "SEBASTIANO?" reverberated under the vast high ceiling.

They swiveled looking for the source of the sound.

"Sebastiano, over here!" a voice called out.

Running toward them was Uncle Tony.

"*Si, si!* Hey, Uncle Tony! Hey!"

They rushed toward each other and embraced.

"Hey! You made it, you made it! How great to see you. Last time I saw you ..."

Sebastiano grabbed Carmelo's arm and pulled him toward Tony. "Tony, this is my friend Carmelo. He's from Riposto, too."

Tony and Carmelo shook hands.

"Good! *Ciao*, Carmelo. Riposto reunion right here in New York City! Come on, let's go. Tell me about your adventures, boys..."

As they made their way walking across the Brooklyn Bridge, the former sailors related their troubles on the *Faleria,* about their fear of conscription, about tricking Rico into giving them passes off the ship, about their stay in Baltimore and the nice lady from Catholic Charities. Tony told them how he had made it to America when life in Italy became unbearable. He had three kids now and lived with his family in a small apartment in southern *Bruculinu.*

"You stay with us until you get jobs. One sleep on the floor and one on the sofa. Maybe take turns."

He told them how he had found a job in the Fulton Fish Market and had been doing relatively well since.

"You Riposto boys can find work there easy.[123] You know fish." "Sure," said Sebastiano. "We can work, get our own place. Thanks, Uncle Tony."

Fished out

BUT WORK AT THE FISH MARKET didn't sit well with the newcomers. For one thing, the hours were difficult. Especially in winter, they didn't like to rise in the middle of the night and make their way in the dark to the smelly market. Though they were young and strong, most of what they did involved lifting and handling heavy crates of fish, which left them tired and sore the rest of the day making it difficult for them to sleep. For another thing, they found they had exhausted their lifelong love of the sea and anything having to do with it.

"Think your uncle knows where else we can get work?" asked Carmelo. "Something away from the water?"

A few evenings later, as they discussed other employment

opportunities, Tony said, "If you don't like it here in the big city, you could try moving out to the country. They got a lot of farmland near Syracuse. They call it *muck*, kind of old swampland. Black earth, very black earth. Good for farming."

Carmelo said farming might be a good change of pace for him. Did Tony have any connections in the farm country?

"Connections? Hey, Carmelo, Italians in America are like a fish net, all tied together. Everybody helps everybody. Remember that when you get set up here and get the chance to help a *paisano*."

"Where is Syracuse from here?" asked Sebastiano.

"Upstate. Any place north of here is Upstate. To New York people, there's only two cities in the state: New York and Upstate. Syracuse is about in the middle. Long way, about 250 miles."

"Maybe we can save some of our wages and take a trip there and look around," said Carmelo.

"Up to you, boys. Lots of Italians find work up there. Sorry I can't get you anything better. Fish work is all I know."

Tony thought about his nephew's situation and mentally scanned his list of countrymen outside of Brooklyn. Most of the Italians he knew were manual laborers, working in the fish markets, factories, and farms. Farms! Ah! He remembered he had heard of an Italian who was a real farmer, one who owned the land he worked on, and hired men to work on it. Tony's wife, Francy, told him it was John Timpano. John had managed to scrape together enough money to buy a large piece of swampland in the Syracuse area from the government.

"He's a muck farmer?" he asked his wife.

"I think he's got some of both, muck and hard," she replied.

"I don't know any Timpano, but I bet your cousin Sal in Cicero[124] knows how to contact him."

"Okay. I'll send a letter."

≈

A few weeks later

SALVATORE REPLIED that, indeed, he knew of a John Timpano who owned a farm on the edge of the Big Swamp near Cicero. The soil there is thick and rich so John had high crop yields. Sal would ask around to see if there might be work for Carmelo and Sebastiano.

A few weeks later, the young men were on a train headed to "Upstate." As they rode along, they tried to remember why the name "Timpano" sounded familiar.

"This guy, John Timpano, must be kinda famous," said Sebastiano. "I mean he *owns* land in America. Not too many Italians—"

"Maybe somebody at the fish market said something about him," said Carmelo.

"Yeah, maybe. But maybe not."

They dropped the subject.

"Lots of farms," observed Carmelo as they passed great expanses of cultivated land.

"Yeah, gotta be work out there. Think you'll miss the ocean?" Carmelo shook his head.

"I've had enough of it. The smell, the mess, the fish—I'm sick of fish. Today I'll take a *finocchio* over a fish. I want to plant *finocchio*[125] like they do in the Old Country. People there who don't live on the coast, they have gardens."

"Don't know about *finocchio,* but I agree with you about seafood. And the whole sea-going life. I'm looking to put down some roots, Melo."

"And you can't put down roots on a ship's deck," he replied. "For roots, you need soil, not steel."

They were approaching Utica. The snarl of tracks as they approached the station caught Sebastiano's eye.

"Railroad's a big business here, Melo. Look at those guys over there slinging big hammers. Bet there's work on the railroad, too."

Carmelo said, "It's good to get away from the big city. Lots of nice things, but too crowded, too busy."

Sebastiano thought for a moment, then said, "And the women are stuck up, too."

Carmelo glanced over to Sebastiano and said, "City women. I don't think they like sailors. Especially ugly ones!"

"Like you!" snapped Sebastiano.

The train took on passengers. A couple of women eyed them as they approached their row.

Sebastiano winked at them. Then flashed his big grin. They looked away and moved on.

Carmelo said, "Such a charmer! A real magnetic animal!"

16 ⋈ Westward Hoe

Onion growing in muck

Muck: the luck of the Italians

WHEN VEGETATION DECOMPOSES in a standing body of water for hundreds of years, the detritus piles up on the bottom. And when the last of the top water is gone, what's left is a deep layer of spongy, black soil that is a bonanza of nutrition for certain desirable crops. It's called "muck." A five-mile area south of Oneida Lake in central New York called the Great Swamp contained a thick layer of this soil and it hosted many farms, also known as mucklands.

In addition to plants, the muck nourished a generation of Italian farmers, who found they could do more than simply work *on* farms, they could *own* them. These mucklands produced so many affluent Italians that soon Italians outnumbered the area's native settlers. By 1925, the Great Swamp area itself became swamped with immigrant Italian laborers looking to work outdoors for good pay.

One Italian mucklander was John Timpano, whose wife, Venetta, was an acquaintance of Francy D'Urso, Tony's wife in Brooklyn.[127]

Venetta had received a letter from Francy asking if there might be work for a couple of young, newly-arrived Italian boys, one of whom was her husband's nephew.

"Sure, sure. Send them along," replied John. "Plenty of work in the fields. We got a new crop of the biggest onions I've ever seen."

≈

Sebastiano gets a sign

STEPPING ONTO THE PLATFORM at the small train station in Canastota, New York, Carmelo and Sebastiano looked for people who might be looking for them.

"Over there, Bas. I think those are our people." Two women, a mother and daughter. The daughter was holding up a sign that read, "Sebastiano."

"*Madonna mia!* Who is that ... that—? "

"Behave," breathed Carmelo.

They approached the two women.

"*Benvenuti* Sebastiano and Carmelo. I am Venetta Timpano, and this is my daughter, Anna.

Carmelo smiled and nodded to Venetta. Sebastiano bowed deeply to Anna.

"Pleased meet you!" he said.

Venetta held out her hand to Sebastiano. "And I... I...over here!"

Sebastiano blinked to attention.

"I am her mother," she snapped.

He bowed, grasped Venetta's hand, and shook it vigorously. "Ah, yes. *Signora* Timpano. My aunt Francy told me about you."

"Good. Your trip went well?"

Both men nodded enthusiastically.

"Beautiful country," said Carmelo.

"Beautiful," said Sebastiano. But he was looking at Anna.

"All right then," said Venetta. "Let's go. My husband, John, is waiting to meet you, and you guys can talk about what kind of work you can do for us."

≈

Job interview

LATER, THE YOUNG MEN TOLD their histories and lineages to John Timpano, who recognized many of the Grassos from the Old Country, including—after the explanation of the name difference— Carmelo's adoptive father, Mariano.

"And how are they, your parents?" asked John.

"I...I haven't been back home since I left, over ten years ago. But...I think they're all right. Oh, I've got a picture. Came just before we left Tony's. Let me show you."

He rummaged in his traveling bag and brought out an envelope. Inside was a picture postcard. On one side of the card was a photograph of Mariano and Maria. He handed it to John.

"Ah, they look good, Carmelo."

He saw Carmelo's eyes were glistening.

"You miss them."

He turned the card over and read aloud the brief message:

> *For my dear son I send this photo as a sign of love, so in*
> *this way you can always remember your dad.*

"Beautiful, Carmelo. So far apart in time and distance, but so close heart to heart. Good for you."

He handed the card back to Carmelo, who stared at the images.

Lightening the mood, John said, "Many Grassos in the world. Many here on my farm, too. You boys have any experience working on a farm?"

They shook their heads.

Carmelo said, "We grew up in a fishing town and went into the merchant marine as soon as we could. All we know is the sea."

"But," interjected Sebastiano, "we're sick of it. Don't want to go on ships anymore. We like the land."

"That's right," agreed Carmelo. He put away the postcard. "We want to learn a different trade."

"So we can live on our own here in America," added Sebastiano.

≈

In the Field

AFTER REFRESHMENTS, John took them outside to look at the land. Under a sheltering tarp at the edge of a large field John bent to pick up an onion from a crate nearby.

"This land is very, very good for onions these days."

He lobbed the onion to Sebastiano.

"Ever see an onion that big?"

"No, never," said Carmelo, flashing back to his galley days many years before. Sebastiano shook his head in agreement.

"The more of these I can pick and sell, the better. They come out of the ground with long stalks. The stalks have got to be cut off."

He picked up a metal shear and snapped it with a sharp twang.

"You cut off the stalks with these—or you can use a jackknife—and put the onion in a crate. You fill a crate and I pay you twenty-five cents. Fair?"

They had no idea, but the work looked easy enough and the prospect of getting any money was exciting.

"You'll need a place to live," said John. "Until you can afford something better in the village, I've got a few of what they call "shanties"[128] on my land. You can live there for a while. You'll have to bunk up with three or four other guys but it's a roof over your head."

"Shanties," repeated Sebastiano."

"If you can last through the winter—do you *Siciliani* know what 'winter' is? Have you lived through a winter in New York state?"

"Cold," stuttered Carmelo, remembering last winter in Brooklyn.

"Gets damn cold here in the Great Swamp. And lots of snow. You'll need warm clothes."

"We have some but will buy more if we need to."

"Yeah, sure. Got stores in town and we'll help you with what you can't find. We take care of our own, boys."

"*Grazie!*"

≈

Divergence

OVER THE REST OF THE HARVEST season, Carmelo and Sebastiano lost the last of their sea legs and became thorough landlubbers. At first, they had progressed together along the same paths, lodging in the village and acquiring personal property. Eventually however, they went in different directions. Carmelo continued working in the fields, moving from farm to farm as the work, and the pay, improved, but Sebastiano got a job with the New York Central Railroad. The two remained good friends over the years, and when Sebastiano finally married John Timpano's daughter, Anna, he asked Carmelo to be his best man.

≈

Go west, middle-aged man

EVEN DIGGING IN THE DIRT was beginning to lose its allure for Carmelo, at least as a way to make a living. Agriculture seemed to suit him. He valued the wideness of the open land, the rich scent of earth, and the companionship of his coworkers. And to his surprise, he discovered he had a talent for growing things.

But despite all the advantages over a life at sea, the pay was simply too little. Even during the deprivations the Great Depression, he had started to develop a taste for the ordinary goods and services the Americans took for granted. Seeing no way to upgrade his life in the farming industry, he began to look for other ways to make a better living. He learned that a big factory in a city a little over a hundred miles to the west was hiring men to work in its foundry. Sebastiano got him a railroad pass so he could take a look around in the city of Batavia where the factory was located. He was astounded by the pay at the Massey Harris tractor parts factory. But the work was hard.

It involved standing near a blast furnace that melted pig iron into a pourable fluid. One of his jobs would be to lug a ladle full of molten iron over to a group of pressed, oiled black-sand molds, and pour the liquid into each until the ladle was empty. Then it was back to the furnace to fill up another ladle and repeat the process, all day long.

Hard work for sure, but the pay! At $750[129] per year, the pay was more than he'd ever received. And there were also "benefits" like holidays and vacations. Though he wasn't as young as when he'd jumped that ship, he was still strong and physically fit from years of outdoor manual labor.

A few weeks later, he said goodbye to his *compari* in the Syracuse area, and moved to Batavia to begin work as a "moulder" in the foundry at Massey Harris.

Availabilities

AS IN THE SYRACUSE AREA, Carmelo found a ready-made Italian community in Batavia. They tended to live on the south side of town, south of the railroad tracks that divided it. But companionship, a social life, help with the intricacies of living in a new place, and more were all available to him as part of the littler Italy there.

Despite his indifference to religion, Carmelo joined St. Anthony's Catholic Church, which was literally an underground church, having been built when the threat of air raids was rampant. (Or that may have been the excuse when funds for a superstructure were lacking.) The services were only vaguely familiar, though they had a certain dramatic attraction. His main interest was in making connections. He was slowly picking up the English language, though it was rife with patois, so his prospects were better within the Italian community that patronized St. Anthony's.

He joined the Holy Name Society, a men's group in the church that held breakfast meetings every three months, where he enjoyed ham sandwiches, donuts, coffee, music, and talks, sometimes even in Italian, by prominent Italian-Americans. These helped him learn how to fit in with the culture and form friendships. He also got to appraise the women of St. Anthony's Children of Mary sodality, who served the food. But being shy, inarticulate, and naive, there was no one he felt he could approach on his own.

Of great help was his friendship with Louis Mancini, a longtime Batavia resident, an American citizen who had served in the US Army in 1917, and was a ready sponsor of Italian immigrants who wanted to become citizens. Louis owned a grocery store that carried many of the traditional items desired by his Italian clientele on the south side of town. He also owned a boarding house on Swan Street[130] in which Carmelo rented a room for twenty dollars a month.

Over the next few years Carmelo managed to save enough money to buy a house. But he wasn't going to buy one and live there alone.

"It's time I got married," he told Louis.

Louis replied, "I'll ask around and see who's available."

17 ⋈ Harder Times

Burdock

"AND HOW MUCH PARMESAN CHEESE do you have?"

Martheana Dreibred,[131] the aid worker, poised her pen over the form.

"That's kind of an intimate question," said Nellie.[132]

"Intimate?"

"Yeah. Nosy. Why do you want to know how much cheese we have?"

Dreibred turned her clipboard to Nellie.

"You're entitled to a certain amount of free cheese every month, but we can't have you hoarding it. I mean, you can't save it up and get the full amount the next month. Some people—no, not you—try to cheat the system and sell off their extra food aid. So I need to know how much cheese you have left so I can put you down for how much you're going to get of your quota from the government."

"Oh. Let me go check."

She went to the icebox and called out, "About half a thing full. Not too much."

Martheana wrote on the form.

"That finishes the list. Sign here. You can pick up your full allotment in about a week. Thanks."

"I hope they're not late with the macaroni and powdered milk. My kid brother eats like a horse."[133]

Martheana closed her briefcase and put on her coat.

"These are difficult times, Miss Cascio. Everyone has to tighten their belt until we're out of this Depression. Even your brother."

"I know. I've told him, but he's a kid, he forgets."

Martheana smiled, and said, "Growing boy. But you're older, you need to explain to him that a terrible thing has happened to the country and it's not like it was when he was younger. Does he work?"

"No, not much. We're trying to keep him in school a little while longer.[134] But I know what you mean about sharing the pain. My mother and father are out every day taking whatever work they can find. It's just hard to get through to him."

At the door, Martheana Dreibred said, "Well, good luck with all that. You'll get a notice when your aid is ready. Goodbye."

≈

NELLIE WENT BACK to knotting together pieces of string and winding them onto a large ball. She had this afternoon off but would be back at the knitting mill early in the morning.

She reflected on the irony of her family's situation. They had fled Sicily in 1910 because of a widespread economic depression and now they were struggling to survive a depression in another country. Back then, there was chaos all over Italy caused by events political and natural. Not only was the economy slow and taxes especially heavy, but adding to the misery, Mount Etna was having fits. Earthquakes, acrid smoke, and fiery skies made life in Polizzi Generosa unbearable.

But at least back then people could leave for better places, like

America. Now, and for different reasons, they were in the grip of another economic catastrophe here in the Promised Land. Though her education had not progressed beyond the eighth grade, she read the papers and magazines that detailed the breadth and severity of the crisis. Even the movies she attended, while she still had nickels to spend, played newsreels showing shocking pictures of people in the big cities looking bedraggled and forlorn as they waited in long lines in the streets outside of soup kitchens.

She teared up as she thought of her parents, now in their fifties, who had never known anything but hard labor, no matter what country they lived in, and could look forward to no easing of the burden. Though life was comparatively easier since coming to America, there was always such a pressing need for funds that the entire family had to work in order to survive. And that was in good times. Now, they were barely able to live on the pittances they earned through the hard labor of everyone in the family—except for Joseph, who would stay in school as long as possible. (Mike had finally learned that men could make better money if they had more education, while women were expected to become mothers so the cost and time for education would be a waste.) As the crisis deepened and spread across America, engulfing the previously comfortable middle class, the government finally got around to doling out surplus food to those in need—which was practically everyone. Some, like her married sister, Frances, even received a stipend to apply toward rent.[135]

The side door flew open and her aunt Rosaria clomped in clenching a bundle of greens in the crook of her arm.

"Good crop today," she said as she deposited the heap in the sink. "That rain last week helped."

Nellie rushed to her and they embraced, then started sorting the greens.

"You sure you got enough for yourselves, Rose?"

"Yeah, plenty. Even got some dandelion in there, but mostly

burdock from near the swamp up the hill in back."

Nellie picked at several small spiny balls that were stuck to the back of Rose's sweater.

"Messy work, Aunt Rose. But thanks for these."

"Couple of eggs and a handful of whatever you got, and you can call it 'Carduni.'"

"Joey won't eat the roots. Says they taste like dirt."

Rose held up a long, dark tuber. "Tell him dirt is good for you. Fills you up and makes you strong."

"Don't give him ideas." said Nellie.

They worked together sorting, stripping the leaves from the stems, cutting off the roots, and washing everything.

"Social worker was here today," said Nellie. "Good thing, too. We're running out of the aid food."

"How much parmesan you got, Natala?"

"Wouldn't *you* like to know," she replied with a grin.

They worked together in silence a few minutes. Then Nellie said, "Sorry to hear about Uncle Matteo's job. Is he doing okay at the salt mine?"

Rose went over to the kitchen table and sat.

"He misses the railroad, but, hey, these are hard times, Natala. We're happy that people still need salt. Nice that he and your papa can work together—when there's work."

"I know," said Nellie. "Papa says it's good to have the work but it's not like the railroad. He's used to being outdoors and not down a thousand-foot shaft with salt dust everywhere."

Nellie dried her hands and came to sit with Rose.

"I read in the papers rich people are jumping out of windows because they lost everything in the stock market. Could it be that bad, Aunt Rose?"

"Loss is painful, Natala. If you're used to something and it's suddenly gone, it hurts. Can even drive you crazy. Nice thing about being at the bottom of the ladder like us, we never had much, so we don't miss much. Gotta work harder, of course, dig greens out of the lawns and creek banks, but we know how to survive. Rich people, to them it's the end of the world. A lot of them can't handle it."

"You're right. If you're poor, there's not a big difference between what you have and nothing. So we keep moving along, hoping tomorrow brings a teeny bit of something more. But if it doesn't, oh well, just another day."

Rose stood up and hugged Nellie.

"Gotta go. Kids home soon and I gotta get my own greens ready for dinner."

Nellie said, "Me, too. Sodality tonight."

"Put in a prayer for us poor souls, Natala. That's the only way we hold up."

"Yes, for sure," said Nellie. "If everybody loved God more and prayed more, we wouldn't have this awful Depression. But even a few people, like the Children of Mary and such, we can lighten the burden on everyone, and especially the ones with faith, faith that God is with us and can help us when we ask Him."

Rose kissed Nellie on the cheek. "Keep the faith for us, Natala. We're so covered in troubles we sometimes lose the light. Not like you. Pray for us, dear!"

"Thank you, Aunt Rose."

"How I wish you had gone into the sisterhood. How blessed would we be to have a real *nun* in the family?"

Nellie dropped her head and shook it slowly.

"I wish it could have been so. I wish. But Mama won't let me, because Papa won't approve, of course. And...and I have some hesitations myself about taking such a big step."

"Like what?"

"Oh, we don't need to discuss it. Private reasons, personal."

Rose eyed her skeptically.

"You in love?"

"Only with God. I just don't think the sisterhood and I are ready for each other right now. Just a personal feeling, you know?"

"All right, then."

"I think there are all kinds of ways to serve God, in addition to being 'on the payroll,' so to speak. Religion is, first of all, a private thing. What you keep in your heart, in your thoughts, and what you do with your life, even if it isn't doing official religious duties."

Rose crossed herself. "I'm glad for that. It means even us 'civilians' can be in touch with the Almighty."

"Yes. We can each be a saint in our own corner of the world."

Nellie escorted Rose to the door.

"I'll pray for our family, Aunt Rose. I'll dedicate this novena to us, to happy days ahead!"

18 ⋈ Run-in

Batavia Daily News, October 17, 1938

"CAR BACKING UP HIT STORE FRONT

Plate Glass Window Shattered by

Machine Containing Rochester Woman"

LOUIS MANCINI WAS HANGING BACCALA in his grocery store when the explosion dropped him by instinct to the floor. The jangle of shattered plate glass and the staccato of bouncing fruit assured him it wasn't a bomb, such as he had experienced in the army. He peered over the meat counter to see the rear end of a 1930 Hudson automobile in place of the cantaloupes and apples he had carefully arranged in the front window.[136] He ran out the door toward the screams of a woman inside the car—on the passenger side. No one was in the driver's seat. He pried open the door and said to the woman, "What the hell? You okay?"

Margaret Sardinia stopped screaming and looked at Louis with startled eyes.

"I don't know, I don't know! The car, the car started backing up and I didn't know how to stop it!"

From across the street, a man came running toward the car.

"Hey, hey! That's my car! What the hell did you do, Marge? You wrecked my car!"

"Fuck your car," said Louis. "Half it's in my store!"

Marge bent to the right and threw up on the street.

"Jesus, lady. You injured? You got blood on your head."

She was babbling.

"She's got shock."

He waved to the man who had come across the street.

"Help me take her into the store."

A small crowd was gathering.

Bill Halsey[137] came around to the passenger side and helped lift Marge out.

"She said she was going to wait in the car for me and our friends."

"You guys been drinking? I smell beer—and fish."

As they brought her into the store and sat her down, Bill said, "We had the fish fry at Yates'. And a couple of beers, yeah."

"I'll call an ambulance," said Louis, and went for the phone behind the counter.

"No, don't bother," Marge said with a great sigh. "I'm okay, I'll be okay. Just shook up a little I guess."

"Okay," said Louis and dialed the police instead.

Another young woman, Helen Recchio, clambered into the store and knelt by Marge.

"What happened, honey? You okay?"

Margaret burst out in tears again.

"Oh, Helen. I'm so sorry, so sorry. This is terrible..."

Helen patted her on the head and dabbed at the cut on the right side of her face.

"It's going to be all right, sweetie."

Marge turned to look at the Hudson and shrieked.

"I can't believe this! I can't believe it! How horrible, how horrible! The car! How am I going to get home?"

"You can stay with us for the night and I'll get ask my dad to drive you back to Perry in the morning."

Louis approached. "You from Batavia?"

She stood and indicated the street.

"Yes, just up Ellicott, on Goade Park.[138] My boyfriend and I were out to dinner with Marge and Bill."

"Says she's from Perry, out toward Rochester?"

"Uh-huh. And Bill's from Rochester. We were celebrating her birthday! What a terrible way to end it. I'm so sorry about your store."

"Gotta get a wrecker here and haul that car out of the way so I can board up the window," he said. "Somebody's gonna get a huge bill for all this."

Helen bent to Marge. "Marge, you're going to miss work."

Marge nodded. "The Mill[139] will get along fine without one sewing machine operator for a day or two."

A pulsing red light alerted them to the arrival of a police car.

OFFICER FRANK RODON[140] thought he'd seen it all, but he made a mental note that he'd never seen the rear end of a Hudson resting in the front end of a grocery store. After determining that the young woman wasn't seriously injured, but mostly drunk, he turned to the car's owner, who was carefully picking his way through the shattered glass and fruit on the floor, inspecting his car.

"Your car?"

"Yes, sorry to say."

"What's your story about how it got here?"

"I didn't see it happen, Officer. I was inside the restaurant, just about to go out the door when I heard the crash."

"What do you think happened?

Bill looked at Marge. "You should probably ask her."

"I tried, but she's not making much sense. Says she was just sitting there when the car revved up and backed out across the street."

Bill smiled, just a bit. "We both know, Officer, that cars don't work that way. She had my keys, so we can guess the rest."

The other policeman, Clarence Bates,[141] approached as he finished writing in his report book. He said, "We're going to have to arrest you both."

"Why me?"

"For allowing an unlicensed driver to operate your car," replied Officer Bates.

"I didn't *allow* her to drive my car! She did it on her own because she had my keys. After dinner she said she didn't feel well and wanted to wait for us in the car. My guess is that she put the key in it to start up the heater—it's chilly tonight. Then she somehow must've hit the gear shifter."

"We'll let a judge decide that, Mr. Halsey. Follow us."

"No! Wait!" cried Helen. "I can put her up. Can she stay at my house tonight?"

"'Fraid not. She's not going anywhere until tomorrow morning after seeing the judge."

"But she has to be at her job in the morning. In Perry."

"Sorry. My job tonight, in Batavia, is to arrest her and hold her for a hearing in the morning. Goodnight, ma'am."

Louis hung up the phone.

"Truck'll be here in twenty minutes," he said to no one in particular. He thumbed through the Yellow Pages for someone to board up his window.

Fred Pulvino,[142] Helen's date, said, "Any way I can help, Mr. Mancini? Where's a broom?"

As he dialed the phone, Louis said, "No, thanks, Freddie." But a moment later, "Well, you can pick up the fruit. Be careful of the glass— hello?"

Someone had answered.

"Hang on."

To Freddie he said, "And lock the door. I'm closed."

≈

The next day

"**WHAT THE HELL HAPPENED**, Louie?" asked Carmelo.

"Ah, kids today, Carmelo, gunghada-gunghada![143] Outta control car drove into my window last night."

"Holy shit! You okay? The store okay?"

"Yeah, fine. Back in business. Whaddya need?"

"Good. The the kids, all right?"

"Yeah."

Carmelo handed him twenty dollars.

"Okay, first, paying my rent. There you are. You got any tripe?"

Louis bent to the case.

"Nope. All out. Some nice calamari, though."

"Hmmmm, I was gonna get some baccala but maybe that's too much fish. How about snails?"

"Snails in next week, Tuesday."

"Okay, gimme the calamari, pound of sausage, and dozen eggs. And I'll get the rest over here."

As he browsed the shelves, Carmelo asked, "Anybody you know?"

"Who?"

"Kids who drove into your store."

"Crazy thing, there was no driver. Girl turned on the car from the passenger seat and must've hit the shift and kicked it into reverse. Backed all the way across from Yates' lot, crossed Swan, up onto the curb and right through my goddam plate glass window."

Carmelo gave a low whistle.

"That's something, Louie. Crazy. Who'd you say the girl was?"

"I didn't. Name's Margaret Sardinia, from Perry. Boyfriend's car, from Rochester."

"Got any *capicole[144]*?" "Yeah."

"Half a pound. And half that of head cheese."[145]

Louis said, "Cops arrested her and her friend, the guy who owned the Hudson," said Louis. "But cops told me the judge let him off this morning[146] because he was inside the restaurant when she started the car. Did you say you wanted some baccala?"

"No. Squid's enough. Looks like you got the place cleaned up okay. Must've been a real mess."

"Young kid I know, Freddie Pulvino, and his girlfriend, helped till late last night."

Carmelo piled his selections on the counter and went to the canned goods section.

"That's nice. Did you know the girl, the girlfriend?"

Louis tore off a large sheet of butcher paper and wrapped the sausage.

"No, but I know her mother from church. Lives not too far from here. The girl wanted to put them up for the night, the guy with the car and the girl who crashed it. But the cops had other ideas."

Louis wrapped the calamari and the luncheon meat and brought them to the counter. Carmelo added a few cans to the pile. Louie started totaling them up.

"So I'm talking with the girl, Helen, as we cleaned up last night. And I thought of you, Carmelo."

"What?"

"You know how you asked me to check on eligible women for you?"

"How old is this girl, Louie?"

"$5.75. Ha! No, not this girl, who's probably seventeen or eighteen. She was saying that her friend, that Marge who crashed the car, works with a woman at the Perry Knitting Mill."

"Oh? Interesting. What's her name?"

Louis took the money from Carmelo, made change, and started putting the items in a shopping bag.

"I think it's Frances. But she's married,"

Carmelo gave the classic Italian gesture for "*What the hell are you talking about*?"

"Louie!"

"This Frances has got a sister. A younger sister, also works at the Mill, but in Mount Morris."

"Oh?" said Carmelo. "And she's not married? How old?"

Another customer entered the store.

"Twenty-five, thirty maybe."

"Kind of old, don't you think? Not married. What's wrong with her?"

Louis greeted the customer, "Hello, Mrs. Recchio. Be right with you."

He bent to Carmelo and murmured in Italian, "And what the hell you know, Carmelo, that's the girl's *mother* over there!"

Carmelo turned and discreetly looked. "The Mount Morris girl?"

"No, the girl who told me about the Mount Morris girl who works with her friend. The sister!"

Louis went around to the meat case and smiled at Mrs. Recchio.

"How you doing today, Marie?"

"Fine."

"Is your daughter all right this morning? She was so nice to stay and help me last night with this, this–" He indicated the boarded-up window.

Mrs. Recchio's face hardened.

"We had a little talk. About carousing. And staying out late."

"Oh, she was so nice, Marie. She wasn't misbehaving. I'm sure of it. Just being helpful."

"I wish she'd hang out with a better class of friends."

"Eh, whaddya gonna do. Kids today..."

Carmelo picked up the shopping bag and headed for the door.

"See you later, Louie."

"Okay. Oh, hey, Carmelo, come over here and meet Marie Recchio. She's the mother of the young lady who knows about the woman in Mount Morris."

Carmelo joined them and nodded to her. "Hello, Please meet you."

"Your daughter," said Louis, "told me about a possible eligible woman in Mount Morris. My friend here is kind of, you know, looking to settle down."

The woman scrutinized Carmelo and then smiled politely.

"Yes, I know the family, not well, but Helen and Marge have mentioned them. Cascio, I believe the name is."

"Cascio," repeated Carmelo. "And there's an unmarried daughter? How old?"

"I really don't know. "

Louis said, "Hey, I can ask around, Carmelo. Don't need to bother Mrs. Recchio now. Thank you, Marie. What can I get you today?"

With a nod to Louis, Carmelo left the store.

19 ⋈ Meet the Parents

Mike and Josephine

LOUIE HELPED CARMELO select two packs of Stogies to add to those he had kept all those years since Baltimore. At some point, he had tried one of the cigars he had bought at the money exchange but found it eye-crossingly strong and disgusting. Yet, he'd heard from Margaret Sardinia's father, Joe, that Mike liked them, so Louie had added them to the gift package of boxed nougat candies Carmelo had bought for Josephine.

"How nice of you, Mr. Tosto," said Josephine. "I like the little boxes."

Carmelo said, "Bite sized! And you can even eat the wrapper around the candy."

He turned to Mike.

"And for you, Mr. Cascio, these."

Mike took the package and sniffed it.

"Ah, I know this. I could smell when you come in the room. Stogies. I like Stogies. You like?"

Carmelo nodded and said, "Sometimes. I smoke Luckies most of the time."

"Cigarette man, okay. How you know Joe Sardinia?"

"His daughter has a friend in Batavia where I live and that girl's family knows a friend of mine," Carmelo replied.

"Hmmmm. And he told you I have a daughter for marriage?" "Not for sure, but I should check. I am looking for a good Italian woman to marry, and Mr. Mancini said you had a daughter who might be someone I should meet."

Mike took out one of the cigars, cut it in half with his jackknife, lit up, and looked Carmelo up and down.

"Where you work?" he asked.

"I got a good job. At Massey Harris."

"In Batavia? What's Messy Hair?

"Tractor parts. Big company."

"And what you do?"

"I work in the foundry. I'm a moulder. Pour pig iron into molds."

"Hard work?"

Carmelo shrugged.

"Make good pay?"

"Pretty good. I save most of it. Want to buy a house someday."

Mike gestured to a chair at the kitchen table.

"Have a seat."

Josephine came back into the room.

"Can I get you something to drink?"

With a twisting wrist motion, Mike pointed to Carmelo. *Aqua. Vino.*"

Carmelo rose and bowed slightly to Josephine. "Ah, *aqua*, if it's not too much..."

"*Vino*," said Mike.

Carmelo looked to Mike. "Sure, some *vino* would be good. Thank you."

Josephine called out, "You know the Macalusos over there in Batavia?"

Carmelo cocked his head and squinted, "No, well, maybe. I've heard the name. I just lately got to know the Recchios. Nice–"

"Sit," said Mike to Carmelo. To Josephine, "He says Recchios and Sardinias are friends."

Josephine came to the table with glasses, a bottle, and a plate of bread.

"You visiting Sardinias?" she asked.

"No," said Mike. "He wants to talk about Natala. Sardinia's daughter is friends with a girl from Batavia."

Josephine asked, "What's her name?"

"Helen, I think. Recchio. I met her mother. Marie, I think"

"Oh, Helen! Helen and Marge are friends. Too bad about the car crash. I'm glad the girl wasn't hurt."

Mike poured.

"Well, funny, that's how I came to know about you folks. And your daughter. Car she was in crashed into the store of my friend Luigi Mancini, who told me about—"

"*Bella Madre!*" breathed Josephine. "Drove a car into a store? How?"

"Said the car backed up by itself," said Carmelo. "Luigi thinks she was drunk."

"Never mind about that," said Mike. "You want to get married to Natala?"

"Yes. I think so. With your permission."

"Does she know?"

"No."

"You want to meet her?"

"Yeah, that's why I came —"

"She's working right now. Come back next Sunday. You like movies?"

Carmelo fidgeted, then shook his head.

"I...I don't understand English too good and they talk too fast..."

"She likes movies."

"Okay."

"You go with her brother, Joe, you three. He'll be *accompagnatore*."

"Okay."

Josephine pointed to a crucifix on the wall. "You go to church?"

Carmelo smiled weakly. "Not much. I was a sailor for many years and, well, not so much church on a ship."

"Oh. Too bad."

Carmelo held up a hand. "But since I started living in Batavia, I go to the church there. Not every Sunday...but I belong to the Holy Name Society and go to meetings."

Josephine started to rise. "You want some cheese?"

"Uh..."

"*Parmigiano*?"

"Uh, sure, thank you very much. If you got enough."

"Natala is very religious, very religious. Maybe you go to church with her next Sunday?"

"Okay."

Carmelo sipped his wine.

"Good vino," he said to Mike, and took another sip.

"You gotta car?" asked Mike.

"No, not yet. I'm saving up for it. There's a '36 Chevy I've got my eye on."[147]

"How'd you get here?"

"Blue Bus."[148]

"You baptized?" asked Josephine.

"I think so. Pretty sure. Yes."

"Where you from," asked Mike.

"Riposto. About ten miles north of Catania."

"What's your father's name?"

"Mariano Grasso."

"Not Tosto?"

"No, Grasso. He adopted me when I was two days old."

"Your mother, she die?" asked Josephine.

"I don't know. They say I was left at a *rota* but no one knows who my parents were. Mariano and his wife raised me as their own and to me they're my real parents."

"That's good to hear," said Josephine. "But sad about your mother."

"Yeah."

"You send them money?" asked Mike.

"Yes. Every month, a little."

"That's good," said Josephine.

"Yes, good," said Mike.

A pause settled in as they each pursued their own thoughts. At last, Carmelo said,

"So...should I come here, to the house, next Sunday?"

"Sure," said Josephine, "High mass is eleven-fifteen. She likes to go to that one."[149]

"You gotta suit?" asked Mike.

"Yes, sir. Where can we go afterward, you know, for lunch?"

"Costas," said Mike.

"Ok."

Josephine rose to clear the table. "You like movies, Carmelo?"

He smiled weakly.

"Uh, like I said, my English...they talk too f—"

"Oh," said Josephine, "yes, I remember. Natala likes movies."

Mike re-lit his Stogie.

"You go anyway. She'll explain," he said.

"Okay."

"Oh, about her name," said Josephine. "At home we say Natala, but outside, everyone knows her as Nellie. You should call her Nellie."

"Okay."

"You like ice cream, Carmelo?"

Carmelo smiled. "Sure!"

"Good. She *loves* ice cream.[150] Tuso's just put in a new soda fountain."

"Okay. Movies and ice cream. I'll be here around ten-thirty next Sunday, then?"

"Make it ten. We can talk a little before you go," said Mike.

"Okay."

A plume of Stogie fumes sliced through Carmelo.

He rose and coughed out, "Well, I should get back to the bus station. It's been nice to meet you, Mr. Cascio, and Mrs."

Josephine accompanied him to the front door.

"Bye," said Mike on his way to the bathroom.

To Josephine, Carmelo said, "Natal--Nellie sounds like a nice girl. See you next Sunday."

20  Facing the Facts

SINCE HIS ORDINATION, James Palmer[151] had identified only with the noun form of the word, *father*, and not the verb. In his youth, however, severe challenges often assailed his vow of celibacy. Eventually his vow triumphed owing to the deeper calling he heard to serve God and the Church as a priest. It helped sustain him during those sometimes-fiery trials, which became mercifully fewer as he aged into his late fifties.

Sex education was always controversial in the Church, and it was barely mentioned in the few counseling courses at the seminary. And yet, as a pastor he was often approached by parishioners for help in working out "intimacy" issues and felt he had not been not sufficiently educated to deliver the kind of help the practicalities of his vocation required. He had turned to books for more knowledge.

Even so, without much real-life experience of his own, he felt under-qualified to help parishioners on the verge of entering the holy sacrament of matrimony. And he was especially squeamish when that parishioner was a young woman.

Like the one pacing the sidewalk outside the rectory today.

Outside

I CAN'T DO THIS," Nellie muttered to herself. "I don't *want* to do this. I don't want to get married. Please help me, God!"

Her mother's voice mentally intruded.

"Natala, you're almost thirty. You've avoided it long enough."

She answered her mother back—more aggressively than she would have dared to if Josephine had been there in person.

"I made up my mind years and years ago. I don't belong with any man. I want to be a bride only to Christ, and he's already right here in my heart, so thank you, Mama. *Basta!*"

"Your older sister married and now it's time for you."

"I don't know what happened there. Frances has been working since she was fifteen, works all the time. Complains she never went on dates, never went to a dance. Told me she doesn't even know what it's like to wear a gown[152]—like I wear gowns all the time, Mama! Ah, so pretty when topping beets!

"I'm getting old and tired. I'd like some grandchildren to enjoy for a little while before I die. Don't break my heart, Natala."

Nellie burst into tears. "I don't want to break your heart. Let Frances give you babies."

She froze in shock at what had leapt out of her. Frances had been married eight years and still hadn't delivered a live baby. "The Cascio curse!" she bellowed. "It's not her fault."

"So, it's up to you now."

"What if I'm cursed, too? You lost six out of nine babies. Do I have to go through that, too?"

"You need to try. You and Frances and Joe came out normal. Rosie, too, but the influenza got her."[53]

Nellie looked toward the rectory. The office light was on. She shouldn't keep the priest waiting.

"Maybe the priest will understand," she thought. "Maybe he'll get a message from heaven and make this right."

She started up the walk again. Then stopped halfway. "Still, he's a *man* and what I need to talk about—" She spun around and strode toward the street again.

"I just can't talk about this....this...stuff. At least not to a *man*. And what about him? How much fun could it be for him to talk to a *woman* about ... about ... that ... stuff!"

≈

Josephine's version

PREVIOUS CONVERSATIONS about "the facts of life" with her mother hadn't allayed Nellie's fears. Josephine's reference to St. Paul's instruction that "wives, submit yourselves unto your own husbands" didn't sit well with Nellie.

"WHAT AM I SUPPOSED TO DO, let him climb all over me?"

The image disgusted her.

"It doesn't last very long. It's like skinning a rabbit: messy at first, but a delicious meal later if you cook it right. Children make it all worthwhile, Natala."

She started to say, "Oh, well, now that you put it that way..."

Instead, she said, "You know I don't like to cook."

"Yes, I know. But maybe you'd be a better mother than a cook. And if you have a son, he'll watch over you and help when you're old—like Joe does now."

"I can take care of you! And besides, Joe doesn't spend much time with us. He's always with that Sophie girl up in Rochester."[154]

"Joe will have a family of his own someday and he can live here with us. Or maybe we can go live with him in a big house in Rochester."

"And so you'll just kick me out? After all these years?"

"No, no. You know we're thankful you've helped out here at home. But a man's a better breadwinner, Natala. Face it, men get better jobs and more pay. Your husband can stay twenty or thirty years at the same job and then retire with money coming in all the time when you're both old."

"Well, that's true. But still, we've been doing all right here."

"Sure, but—"

"Mama, I do not want to get married! Don't make me do it! Don't allow it to happen! It would be awful."

"Natala! Natala! Calm down. Listen to me. You're a woman. We've got to live according to our bodies. Sure, you can pick string beans, top onions, even run a sewing machine, but that's just part of you. A woman...a real woman is...can do so much more. More than a man can do. Men are stronger, sure, so they can work at the harder jobs. But a woman, you Natala, a woman is made for motherhood."

"Nuns are women, made for motherhood, too, but they don't have husbands—and babies."

Josephine's face hardened.

"You are not going to be a nun. You told me yourself."

"I have good reasons to not go live in a convent."

"Yeah? Like what?"

"I told you. It's...it's...personal, private. I don't have that kind of...I don't have what's called a 'vocation,' a clear calling from God to go live in a convent."

"All right then."

"But I can live like a nun outside of a convent. I can still be pure, and prayerful, and be active in the Church like I am. What's wrong with serving God like that?"

"You can do both as a wife and a mother. A nun makes a great sacrifice, the ultimate one for a woman. But not every woman can be a nun, I mean, not everyone gets the call, like you said. If you don't, then you need to be a full woman. God made you a woman so you can produce children. You're just being selfish, because you're always so oversensitive.

"Something doesn't feel right about that, Mama, but I can't find a way to say it." After a moment, she said, "Anyway I can't imagine why anyone would want to marry me."

"There was that nice young man from Rochester. He really liked you, and I could tell you liked him too, at least more than some of those other guys that came sniffing around. He seemed harmless enough."

"Richard. Yes, he was nice. But...he had some...shortcomings—I *mean, nothing came of it anyway."*

Josephine looked out the window and shook her head slowly.

"I wonder what happened there. You won't tell me about that either."

"Nothing to tell!"

"Anyway, there are more Richards out there. One will come around someday. Let me remind you, time is running out, Natala. We must find someone."

"Just so you can have babies to play with?"

"So you don't wind up sorry for the rest of your life. So you're not an embarrassment to your family. I don't want to be the one they say has a spinster daughter."

"So, that's all I am, and all I can be? Just a wage earner or an embarrassment? Oh, Mama, it hurts, that you feel that way about me!"

"No, that's not all you can be. Like I said, you can give me a son-in-law. You can be my married youngest daughter, and mother of many."

"I guess I'll never make you understand."

"See the priest."

≈

With the priest

The rectory door opened.

"Father Palmero?"asked Nellie.

"Uh... no—"

"Or is it Palermo?"

"Uh, neither. It's Palmer. Father Jim Palmer. Come in. Miss Cascio?" "Nellie?

Glancing at the slip of paper in her hand, she said, "Oh. I must have written it down wrong. Somehow, I thought there'd be an Italian priest. I heard we had a new assistant. Is Father Grasso[155] away for long?"

Palmer ushered her into the office.

"It'll be a while. First, there's the retreat, then some official business with the Archbishop in Buffalo. Please make yourself comfortable, have a seat."

"He's the one I usually see. Where were you before Mount Morris?"

"Oh, I'm just mostly over in Piffard. I kind of shuttle between several churches here in Livingston County and Geneseo. Would you like some water?"

Nellie left her jacket on but smiled at the priest. "Oh, yes, that would be nice."

He poured from a pitcher at a side table.

"Father Grasso left me a note that you were seeking some premarital counseling?"

Nellie accepted the glass and took a sip.

"Premarital. Yes, I guess it's pre. I just got engaged and the girls at the Sodality said I should. My mother, too."

Palmer took his seat behind the desk and picked up a pen. "Marriage is a holy sacrament," he said. "Blessed by our Lord Himself at Cana. You're familiar with the story?"

"Yes, Father, I know all of them and have known them since I was a little girl."

"That's wonderful! You realize, don't you, that the Church has an important interest in supporting the marriages of its members, an obligation to help keep them on the highest spiritual level. And, of course, we want to help them be happy, too."

"Oh, yes. And that's what I'm determined to do, Father. Some of the non-Catholic girls I work with just go off and get married as though it's just another...another, I don't know, *fling*?"

"I'm impressed with your piety. But tell me, usually we give counseling to couples. Is there a reason why your fiancé isn't with you today?"

Nellie squirmed and took another sip of water.

"Well," she wheezed, cleared her throat and began again.

"Well, two things. One, my fiancé doesn't know English too

well—he came here from Italy just a few years ago. I'll bring him another day, but first I thought I'd speak with a priest about some things that I'm wondering about."

After a long pause, Palmer said, "I see. What kinds of things?"

"I've always tried hard to be a modest woman, Father. When my girlfriends would talk about vulgar things, like about fooling around with men, you know, like flirting, telling dirty jokes and stuff... "

She paused and squirmed in her chair, looked out the window, cleared her throat and continued.

"...well, I wouldn't stick around. I'd turn on my heels and get away from that kind of thing. In case you don't know, I'm a member of the Sodality here, and I take very seriously the Sodality promise I made to '...*keep myself pure and innocent, and to avoid the occasions of sin.*' I don't look at dirty pictures, I don't show off my body, and that sort of thing. Modesty. Chastity. That's the right thing to do, isn't it?"

"Purity is certainly a virtue, an important virtue, and you're right, many people these days don't value—"

"Right. Right. But the problem with that is ignorance. I never thought much about it, never missed it because I never expected to get married—never even *wanted* to get married. But now—"

A worried look came over her face. Tears formed.

"But now...now I'm about to get married and I know there are things I don't know. Things everybody else seems to know. Know what I mean?"

"Miss Cascio, do you mean sex? Sexual relations in marriage?"

Nellie stood up quickly.

"Maybe, maybe this is something I should wait to talk to Father Grasso about."

"He'll be away for a several weeks."

"Yes. Right. Or maybe an older priest."

Palmer rose, too.

"Of course, of course, whatever makes you feel more comfortable. But I think I can handle it. Has your mother spoken to you of these things? That's usually who—"

"She doesn't have much to say. Just put up with it, she says. For her, it's all about the babies."

The priest gestured toward her chair and sat at his desk again. "Please, have a seat and don't be afraid. And, by the way, I'm older than Fr. Grasso, plenty old!"[156]

Nellie gave a quick laugh and sat down.

"And besides, in seminary we get some training in counseling. It's part of the ministering we do as servants of the Lord, who sanctified the institution of marriage. But if you're not comfortable with me—"

"Oh, no. No, you're not the problem. It's *men*—I mean, *me*, me! My mother says I'm oversensitive."

"That's all right. I'm here to help. Would you like some more water?"

Nellie nodded.

"Here you are. May I call you Nellie?"

"Sure. Everyone does."

"Before we go on, Nellie, I want to assure you that our conversation is totally confidential. Like in the confessional."

"I have not sinned, Father!"

"I know, I know. I just wanted you to know that whatever we say here stays here. So, you—and I—can speak freely, without fear of incurring judgment or criticism."

"Uh-huh."

Back at his desk, Fr. Palmer took up two booklets.[157] He glanced at one.

"Maybe we should start with the basics, Nellie. What do you know about the physiology of human reproduction?"

"The what?"

"Physiology. How the body works?"

"Not too much. Just that a man and a women, you know, get together, do it, and nine months later a baby comes out."

"Well, that's right, in a general way, very general way. The Creator has designed us—even the animals—in very specific ways to reproduce. I think it would help for you to know at least the basic process—"

"Well, I think I've got a pretty good idea. I've seen dogs, you know, together. Like that."

"But the internal processes, what goes on inside the body that makes it all happen so a child can develop there. Do you know how that works?"

"Do I have to?"

"Not really. God has made it so that His plan functions even without our knowledge."

"Thank you, God," Nellie whispered to herself.

Palmer continued, "But people aren't like the animals in a certain, important, way. We have minds, we can have understanding, we can know about things even when we don't have to know about them."

"Then why know about them?"

"Because sometimes people feel uncomfortable with what they don't know. You said it yourself, innocence can lead to ignorance, which makes you fearful. Understanding often quiets fear."

"What if a person doesn't want to know?"

"Then they get so upset they come to a priest for comfort when they're about to get married and don't know what's about to happen to them."

After a long pause, Nellie said, "I see what you mean. Fear. That's me. I'm fearful. Yes, because I really don't know what's going to happen to me."

She leaned toward the desk.

"So what's going to happen? After I get married."

Palmer held up one of the booklets.

"Well, I can try to explain it so you won't be embarrassed or fearful. But I got you some reading material that you can study in private—you do read, don't you?"

"Oh, yes. I like to read."

"Then take these booklets, they're published by reputable medical sources—and are approved by the Church. Take them and read up on the 'physiology' of reproduction. You might have questions after you read them, but you can come back and we can discuss them until you understand. How does that sound?"

"Do they have pictures?"

Palmer opened to one of the pages that displayed a drawing of a female body. It was the most minimal of depictions, mostly an outline with arrows pointing to various places on the form. He turned the page to a similar drawing of a male body. Nellie quickly turned away.

"Do I have to look at things like that?"

Palmer smiled.

"It's probably easier than looking at the real thing for the first time."

Nellie gasped.

"These pictures and the explanations are meant to introduce you to the things you should know, but they do it in a very plain and educational way. And again, you can study them in private. Knowledge, Nellie. Knowledge leads to understanding, leads to a lessening of fear. I think you'd feel better with a little more knowledge."

"I see what you mean. Maybe. I don't know."

Palmer picked up the other booklet.

"And this one," he said showing her the cover, "this one, goes over some of the same material as the other one but goes more into relationships. Sometimes it's called 'psychology.' So, the first book is about the 'physiology,' the physical or the body, and this one is about the mental, or psychological. Most of the time when parishioners come in for counseling, it's about the psychological aspects of the marital relationship. How to get along better, how to resolve problems, especially about sex."

Nellie sat back quickly.

Palmer leaned toward her.

"How do you get along with your fiancé, Nellie? Do you enjoy each other's company?"

She looked out the window.

"We hardly know each other. My parents arranged it."

"Ah, well, that happens a lot in our Italian communities. But surely your parents want you to be with someone who is...who is, shall we say, compatible?"

"I don't think they care about such things. As long as he isn't poor, or a criminal, or a cripple any man will do."

"What's his name? Your fiancé."

"Carmelo."

"And he's from the Old Country? How long has he been in this country?"

"Ten years or so."

"How old is he?"

"Around thirty-seven, I think."

"Hmmm...that's kind of—"

"*Old*, don't you think? That's what I said to my mother."

"Has he been married before? Is he divorced?"

"No, I don't think so. He was a sailor for many years, lived mostly on a ship. Had a girlfriend once, in Turkey, but that didn't work out. I think she left him or something. He cries when he talks about it. Since he's been in America he's been working on farms, mostly over in the Syracuse area, trying to get established. Now he works in Batavia at a factory."

"Ah, so, in a sense, he's really just getting started. And you, may I ask your age?"

"Twenty-eight."

"Hmmm...quite an age difference, about ten years. "

"Nine."

"Okay. Most women are married by your age. Not that there's anything wrong with that, just..."

"I know, another psychology thing. Like I told you, I never thought I'd get married. So here I am in this pickle, about to get married but knowing nothing about being a wife, not to mention a mother!"

She started to sob. "God help me!"

Palmer went over to her and patted her on the shoulder.

"There, there, Nellie. God is right here with you. With both of us."

"Uh-huh. Yes, I know. And He will save me from all this, won't He?"

"Yes."

"I... I should go home now."

He embraced her.

"Take your books, Nellie."

21 ◄ Convergence

Part 1

Picket Line Post
ITEM
September 22, 1939

"Mr. and Mrs. Bartolo Cascio have sent invitations for the marriage of their daughter, Nellie, to Carmen* Tosto, to take place at the Church of the Assumption tomorrow at 9 o'clock. A reception will be held later at St. Anthony's Church Hall, Batavia."

*sic

Part 2

Picket Line Post
ITEM

"TOSTO-CASCIA*

The Assumption Church was the scene of a
pretty wedding Saturday morning when Miss Nellie
Cascia* became the bride of Mr. Carmen* Tosto of
Batavia. The ceremony was performed by the Rev.
Dominic J. Grasso, pastor of the church, in the
presence of a large number of friends and
relatives.

The bride, given in marriage by her father, wore a gown of heavy satin, trimmed with orange blossoms. Her veil was trimmed with orange blossoms and a crown of rhinestones, and she carried a bouquet of orchids.

The maid of honor was Miss Mary Andolina, and she wore an old-fashioned gown of peach corded taffeta en bustle, with matching accessories. She carried a colonial bouquet of Talisman roses.

The bridesmaids were Miss Margaret Sardinia and Miss Helen Rechio* of Batavia. They wore gowns of heavy taffeta with combining accessories, and carried arm bouquets of red roses.

The best man was Carmen DePlato* of Batavia.

The ushers were James and Matthew Joseph Tripi* of this village.

Later in the day there was a reception at St. Anthony's Church Hall, Batavia. After Sept. 30, Mr. and Mrs. Tosto will be at home in Batavia.

Pre-nuptial events were a variety and kitchen shower given by Miss Mary Andolina of Mr.* Morris, Miss Margaret Sardinia of Perry and Miss Helen Rechio* of Batavia."

*sic

Part 3

Batavia Daily News

"**TOSTO**—At St. Jerome's Hospital on December 23 1940, to Carmelo and Nellie Tosto of No. 233 South Swan street, a son, named Mariano."

Fine [The End]

The story is *finita*. More about the book follows.

Postface

The backstory

SICILIAN GOTHIC IS A NOVEL about my parents that culminates with me. What follows is a short essay about *Sicilian Gothic* and the book's "parent," me. A preface usually contains an overview of the coming story and some notes about how to read it. And an epilogue continues the story from the perspective of the story itself. This "postface" is mostly a commentary outside of the world of the story, but connected with it. It's a brief account of how I came to write the book.

Fully retired

WHEN I LEFT MY POST-RETIREMENT JOB at an Apple store in northern California at the age of seventy-four, I stared at a future without friends and family nearby. For the previous seven years, my coworkers—almost half of whom were younger than my oldest grandkids—had been such a good substitute for community that, like a fish that doesn't know when it's in water, I didn't appreciate the role they fulfilled. Once I was permanently separated from my fifteen hours a week immersed in that store's "Cheers bar" environment ("where everybody knows your name, and they're always glad you came"), I felt mental asphyxia setting in.

I knew I was considered "old," but I now felt it keener than ever. But in the ten years we'd lived in California, we still had only one or two local friends, didn't belong to any social organizations, didn't even know our neighbors. Almost all of my family—kids, siblings, and other relatives—lived far across the country to the east. A bleak future loomed ahead. Everything I'd read about aging insisted that community was essential to forestall a lethal descent into decrepitude.

"Go east, old man," said all the signs. Not something I'd ever expected to do. But the impending bleakness flipped a switch. We had to move. We went from an otherwise comfortable home in liberal northern California to one of the deepest of Red dis-united states, Georgia. Be it ever so humbling, there's no home like a place you never would've imagined moving to.

As it turned out, it was the best decision. We have more friends, more politically compatible friends, and more inspirational resources than anywhere since Minnesota.

The two-year trial

FROM OBSERVATIONS OF MY OWN and of others' major life transitions—retirement, relocation, change of marital or health status, etc.—there's about a two-year period before a new normal emerges. That period is filled with conscious and unconscious experimentation, while you search for fertile ground in which to grow again.

For me, long-form writing became a major preoccupation. I wrote a ninety-five thousand-word memoir about my entrance into and exit from a creepy religion. But after two years of massaging those words, I was tired of the material and decided to take a break from writing about myself, especially about such a distressingly misspent life.

That's when the idea for this book emerged.

As a writer, my "big bang" moment came when I saw an item in an old marine journal announcing the impending construction of the very ship my father escaped from in Baltimore in 1925.

The very obscurity of this item blared its importance to me—kind of like seeing yourself in the background of a TV news story. How many people in the world can say, "hey, that was my dad's ship!" It's the ship he listed on his naturalization application, the one on which he spent an important part of his life. The man, who had been so mysterious to me when I was growing up as his son, had inadvertently left evidence of his existence on earth long before he became my father (and nemesis). It was almost as if he were alive again, but at enough distance where I could safely observe and appraise him. And as I discovered more evidence of his existence, I came to like him even more than when I last saw him in 1975, the year before he died. By then, our relationship had become more cordial, though far from close. I was older and somewhat wiser, and he was older, frailer, and less intimidating. In writing his story I found myself having to invent character traits and incidents for which I had little or no documentable evidence. In so doing, I, in a sense, have re-created him in my own likeness. Like son, like father.

My mother left much more evidence as she flowed through the various institutions that attended her fifty-year life in America and on earth. I was excited to see a copy of the Ellis Island immigration logbook listing my grandparents, my aunt, and my own newborn mother as passengers on a ship named the SS *Venezia* in June 1910. I soon discovered a photo of that ship and the birth records of people in my grandparents' Sicilian home town of Polizzi Generosa. I thirsted for even more knowledge.

As I uncovered more facts about these people, I realized there still weren't enough details, especially about my father, to constitute a simple, objective biography. The fact that my father was a foundling and thus had no traceable genealogy, cloaked him in more of a mystery than when I knew him. Instead of letting the mystery be, I imagined several plausible scenarios to fill in the gaps between the facts that could be documented.

Though I had always considered myself a writer, short forms were usually my genre. These included advertising copy, jingles, pop songs, and blog essays. I had written a couple of short stories, and even a play, a great many years ago, but the story of Carmelo and Nellie now seemed tellable only with the connective tissue of fiction.

This couldn't have been possible, at least not by me, prior to the internet. It's sobering to consider what people in the distant future will be able to document about people living in this era—assuming they'd be interested. But for those living after the turn of the twentieth century, it was almost unimaginable that someone in the twenty-first century could see the ship manifests, immigration records, census records, newspaper stories, letters, and a host of other artifacts that can now be accessed by the diligent researcher. I now had a trove of facts to which I could tie much of the narrative about my progenitors.

This project occupied me beginning in early 2018, and while it is a first novel and probably has all the flaws typical of first novels, I console myself knowing that for my family, at least, it could be a resource for their own origin stories.

Beyond legacy

BUT WRITING THIS BOOK has become even more than that. As the writer Haruki Murakami suggests, even novelists can do something to resist the frightfully declining state of our world.

> *What I can do is to write good fiction. After all, when I write a good story, good fiction, we can understand each other if you are a reader and I'm a writer ... There's a special secret passage between us, and we can send a message to each other. So I think (writing good stories) is a way I can contribute to society ...* [158]

I've become pessimistic about the future, with Mussolini-wannabes popping up at home and abroad. Climate change is the great leveler that will reduce civilization to the lowest degree of viability—at best. It may be too late. Or maybe not. With those odds, I laud those who fight for sustainability in an unalterably declining environment. I'd like to be more of an activist than I am. Though I unite in spirit with those who are working to save civilization, those who are able to take to the streets, start petitions, even run for office in order to make America sane again (well, okay, saner). I'm grateful to them, as we all should be. But I can contribute in other ways: by voting, giving financially to relevant causes, participating in discussion groups, and the like. These are more within my capabilities these days. And now, buoyed by Murakami's insight, I feel I'm entitled to offer my writing, such as it is, with this novelized biography in support of a hopeful future. Here's why.

Both my parents were immigrants. Yes, there were prejudice and inequality, as there are with most new immigrant groups. But there was also opportunity and a legal framework within which they could live and work and eventually become full-fledged Americans. They made it—both parents became naturalized citizens. Sure, they had desire, persistence, families and friends for support. But they also had a social and governmental system that allowed for their development. It's a shame that a too-large segment of America as of this writing has become, once again, more xenophobic and hostile to immigrants, denying the country the richness of immigrant potential, and leading to the hardening of the American heart.

Perhaps this simple story of two simple and innocuous people can soften those hearts somewhat and help readers encourage their leaders to see the light. For the sake of those who have the most to gain from such enlightenment, my grandchildren and their children, I hope so.

Mario Tosto
May 2019

For Images & Insights about this book, visit siciliangothic.com

Acknowledgments

EVEN IN THE GUISE OF "FICTION," with its attendant creative license, researching family history is a lot easier when there are living people who can answer the hundreds of questions a writer would have in order to fill out a convincing story. The time period of this novel is 1901 to 1939, and there are almost no first-hand witnesses left to query, especially about the earlier years. That's why it's been especially wonderful to have some of the materials that have been shared with me by family members.

Sources

AS MENTIONED, A MAJOR ASSET was a 1978 audio recording of recollections by my Aunt Frances Guarino, made by my brother, Carmen. This helped supply details about my mother's experiences when she lived in Mount Morris, New York between 1910 and 1939. He and his wife Pat also returned a review version quickly, which I appreciated.

My father's history is a lot murkier owing to his foundling origin, his youth in a Sicilian fishing village, and later years aboard ships. Fortunately, there is an audio recording made in 1984 where I interview his adoptive sister, Concettina Grasso Mandolia. One always wishes the recording could be clearer, the questions more probative and wider ranging, and could have included some of the incidental details that can give a story a rich setting. But, alas, all I have is what's recorded on micro-cassette cartridges. In any case, much of the details about Carmelo's early life came from that recording.

A 1999 letter from Leonarda "Lee" Grasso Fraker gave some important information about Carmelo's time in the Syracuse, New York area. His best friend, Sebastiano Grasso, had a relative who lived in Brooklyn, who was apparently instrumental in getting the two young ex-sailors jobs on the muck farms in the Great Swamp area near Lake Oneida. Lee's mother was Anna Grasso, who was the daughter of John Timpano, who owned a large farm in the area. Anna was also the wife of Carmelo's best friend, Sebastiano.

Even with the invaluable aid of several personal recollections, this book could not have been written without the powerful search tools available today. One of the most useful tools was referred to me by Ms. Holly C. Watson, Deputy Livingston County (NY) Historian. It's the website, fultonhistory.com. As she says of it: "It's a slightly quirky site but often quite helpful."

"Quirky" indeed! An interface straight out of the 90s, but gloriously packed with what it claims are "44,000,000 Old Newspaper pages from US & Canada." Once you figure out how to use its (hidden) Boolean search function, selected pages display as PDFs. This was the tool I needed in order to discover not only some essential facts but much of the minutiae about life in Mount Morris (Tuso's new soda fountain) and Batavia (the Mancini store car crash), publications that are not covered in depth by the big boys like *newspapers.com*. And it's free. Makes me grateful my folks and I came from small towns with newspapers (without which there'd be no record of my First Grade beanbag prowess).

Readers

Charlotte Guarino Harcleroad Frances's daughter, lives in Mount Morris. She has been invaluable in tracking down bits of local history, adding her own memories and photos of my mother's early life. She consulted with the local historian and others to answer my questions and secured a local author's book on the history of the Assumption Church. She's been enthusiastic about this project from the beginning.

Mariagrazia Caruso, is a distant cousin who resides in Catania, Sicily and is fluent in English and other languages. She lives next door to her grandmother, Maria, who is the daughter of Carmelo's adoptive sister, Concettina. Using email and WhatsApp, we've explored several areas of family history. Though she's also advised me on the Italian language and culture, any mistakes are wholly my own.

Laurie Halsey Tosto, my daughter-in-law, is a meticulous proofreader/copy editor who, on several occasions, gave cheerfully of her time to comb through these thousands of words. She has a scrupulous eye for detail—can spot a typo at fifty paces—and is an expert wielder of search tools that turned up several obscure items. Very useful. Any typographical or syntactical errors were introduced by me after her review. I have appreciated her perspective as someone who never knew Mel and Nel nor their immigrant communities. It has been a valuable lens on the narrative.

Carmen Tosto, my brother, in addition to supplying the recording for the core data of this story, has also been helpful in reviewing the chapters as I've finished them, often adding items of local history and corrections. I've enjoyed writing bits I know will crack him up. His wife, Pat (née Grasso), was a welcome cheerleader as he shared my drafts with her.

Clare Petersen, my daughter, has been looking in on my drafts from the beginning and made several helpful comments. I added some items to the story based on her suggestions. She also advised on and helped produce the artwork for some of the chapters.

Bart (Richard) Tosto, my brother, graciously gave me the benefit of his thirty-year career as a high school English teacher by reviewing some early drafts. While I mostly ignore his warnings. About sentence fragments. I value most of his other editorial suggestions. I appreciate that he has another name I could borrow for this story (see endnote 108).

Robert Prickett, a new friend acquired through the marriage of my grandson, Nick. His interest in and critiques of my writings have encouraged me. He suggested I try historical fiction and was enthusiastic about my early drafts of this book. Sadly, he passed away before he could read the full manuscript.

Susan Webb is a longtime friend who knows little of my family but knows me pretty well otherwise. It's been helpful having her look through this narrative and provide responses to the story at various points. Her eagle ear alerted me to some glitches in the audiobook, which I was able to correct before publication.

Peter Tosto, my son, whose teaching skills, patience, and coding expertise got me through the e-book manuscript preparation phase. He's a good teacher and an excellent son. May his sons treat him as well as he has treated me. It was his idea to produce the audiobook version. The reason you're reading this now is that as I continued to polish this manuscript, he convinced me to apply the software programmer's motto to art: It's never finished; it's just abandoned.

Joan Ostrin, my wife, reviewed countless drafts and asked probing questions that helped me clarify and augment the story. Lucky for me, she's readily available whenever I ask her to "taste this" as I try out ideas. In the audiobook, she is the voice of young Nellie in Chapter 10, and of the society page reporters in the "Convergence" chapter. I'm especially grateful for her sympathy and forbearance on this book while I (with Peter's help) prepared the e-book and print manuscript during long episodes of HTMHell.

Though my offspring do not carry her genetic imprint, I know they agree with me that their lives and characters owe much to her influence over the past forty-seven years.

NOTES

For information beyond these notes, visit siciliangothic.com

[1] There is plenty of documentation about this practice. Additionally, a family member from Sicily affirmed that Carmelo was left at a "*rota.*"

[2] From 1198 the first foundling wheels (*ruota dei trovatelli*) were used in Italy; Pope Innocent III decreed that these should be installed in homes for foundlings so that mothers could leave unwanted children in secret instead of killing them , a practice clearly evident from the numerous drowned infants found in the Tiber River. https://en.wikipedia.org/wiki/Baby_hatch

[3] Invented character

[4] Not documented

[5] These were often women who had already given up their infants to the facility, and this task was a kind of "payment."

6 Name of a high school teacher known for her fierceness as a destroyer of the squirt guns she confiscated during class.

[7] "First"

[8] "Lucky"

[9] "Shiny"

[10] "Full moon"

[11] "Knock"

[12] The custom in Sicily was that women kept their fathers' names even after marriage.

[13] A music notation term meaning "quickly." See https://musicterms.artopium.com/t/Tosto.htm

[14] Most likely, he was baptized but I haven't determined where and when from baptismal records of any of the churches in Riposto at that time.

[15] Related to me by Carmelo

[16] Apocryphal story, part of family lore

[17] Apparently, a facility that received foundlings got to choose their official surnames

[18] From interview with Concettina Mandolia, Carmelo's adoptive sister

[19] Quoted in 1984 recorded interview with Concettina

[20] A lifelong practice

[21] aka Able-Bodied seaman. There is some family lore that says he got to be a Navigator, but I'm dubious about this. The official position required much more training and experience than he would have had. However, to go from a below-decks job, such as in the galley, to working topside as an "AB" is plausible. An AB may work as a watchstander, a day worker, or a combination of these roles.
See: https://en.wikipedia.org/wiki/Able_seaman

[22] "SS" stands for "Screw Ship," indicating the propeller method of water propulsion. I imagine some disgruntled passengers in steerage may have had a more pungent description

[23] Stated on Nellie's naturalization application, June 27, 1936.

[24] Per ship manifest from Ellis Island files

[25] I know he played guitar, but this story is a fabrication.

[26] Frances said he used to travel as far as Cefalu to fetch wood, but it's over 40 miles away so I think she was exaggerating or mistaken. Yet, fetching firewood was a thing anyway.

[27] Speaks more of my experience as a guitar-playing dude in my small circle of friends.

[28] Gleaned from first-person accounts in the Ellis Island oral history files

[29] Records from Polizzi Generosa: Bartolomeo's mother was a Giampapa. Giuseppa was probably a cousin on his mother's side of the family.

[30] Based on my personal memory of the upstairs bedroom we kids slept in on overnight stays with the grandparents. My brother,

Carmen, corroborates and says it's still in the family, with one of our cousins. I wonder if they still have the chamber pot

[31] True

[32] A popular nickname for that railroad, celebrated in song "Where do you work a John, On the Delaware Lackawan..."

[33] This may have been Roseanne Trippi

[34] No documentation on this, but it has long been part of the Tosto lore that Carmelo was friends with the captain of the ship he worked on. How a lowly sailor could become a buddy of the captain is a mystery to me, but I'm going with the story. I gave them the same city of origin, Catania. His surname was a common one in Batavia, New York where I grew up. It was originally going to be Mancini, which would have made a little joke with the first name. But I need the name for a real person later in the story.

[35] His height was 5' 3"– same as Nellie

[36] The Liomi story was related by Carmelo several times to various family members. There's no other documentation.

[37] *spianare la strada*

[38] Based on a personal experience of mine when a young teen, on singing a hymn about the Virgin Mary in school

[39] The song describes loneliness and loss represented by the Black Earth, all that is left after devastation.

[40] He stayed in school only until he could be a substantial help to Mariano's fishing work. He probably didn't go further than what we would call second or third grade. Even later in life, he couldn't do much more than sign his name.

[41] "Do not forget me," a song title.

[42] My sister-in-law, Jody Tosto, recalled the time Carmelo told his story of Liomi, during which he sang this song, "Non Ti Scordar," and Jody joined in. Many recordings of the song exist today, Pavarotti's rendition being one of my favorites.

[43] There is no proof either way.

[44] Invented for this story. There is no evidence.

[45] That he was barred from ever seeing Liomi again is part of Carmelo's story.

[46] See: https://context.reverso.net/translation/italian-english/tosto

[47] This was a real person, a close friend of Carmelo's, though all the dialog is invented.

[48] Suggested by a ship's manifest showing the number of meals served to Natala, my infant mother. When travelers paid the shipping company, they not only were entitled to cram themselves into steerage with 1800 other passengers, but also a certain number of meals per day. Because my mother was a newborn infant when they boarded the ship, the family was not assessed for her feeding, since it was assumed she'd be nursed by her mother. But with a history of nursing problems, probably owing to the genetic problems associated with inbreeding, the infant had to be fed, probably with some kind of supplemental formula. My Aunt Frances, in a recorded interview related that they tried to give her regular food but she wouldn't take it. This is when Francesca was impressed to see her first banana. Each extra meal provided by the ship was recorded so the family could be billed for it. The only "meals" listed were for the baby.

[49] Josephine's naturalization application

[50] The *Venezia* picked up passengers in Naples before loading the Sicilian customers at the port of Palermo. Both cities would have been points of departure for travelers from the Western European continent and North Africa, suggesting there must have been a variety of languages spoken among the passengers of the *Venezia*.

[51] A direct quote from the Ellis Island oral history files

[52] These descriptions come from the Ellis Island online library and from comments in the Oral History archives.

[53] Not directly attributable to her, but general information on

immigration procedures at Ellis in 1910 give much of this information.

[54] Likely Public Charge

[55] Real person, name written in ship's ledger

[56] Franciscans are considered a mendicant order that relies on alms

[57] "Ouch!"

[58] My invention

[59] Probably manganese, which was extensively mined in the Genoa area at the time

[60] Entirely invented

[61] Able-bodied Seaman

[62] A statement he used in a speech in 1927: *"Rendi l'Italia grande di nuovo."* See: https://solini-told-immigrants-america-great-article-1.2725269

[63] King of Italy since 1900. See: https://en.wikipedia.org/wiki/Victor_Emmanuel_III_of_Italy

[64] Mussolini coined the term *fascism* from the *fasces* carried before Roman magistrates. These were the ancient Roman symbol of the life-and-death power of the state, bundles of the lictors' rods of chastisement which, when bound together, were stronger than when they were apart.

[65] No documentation about this; an inference from comments made by Italian family suggesting Carmelo had a connection in America. It was probably through Sebastiano.

[66] Probably homemade

[67] A coastal town about forty miles northeast of Polizzi Generosa

[68] Not unusually, there was another family named Trippi who lived down the street. They had been Rosaria's and Matteo's sponsors five years before. Related by my cousin, Charlotte, who still lives in Mount Morris. Also, corroborated by census records.

[69] Per census record

[70] My conjecture

[71] Sung by Canisius College Glee Club, Buffalo, New York, circa 1962. My first and only involvement with choral singing until 2018

[72] Information found by my cousin, Charlotte

[73] Most of his employment information is contained in census records

[74] Founded by a man named Foster, who named the town after the backward spelling of his name

[75] See: https://en.wikipedia.org/wiki/Room_and_pillar_mining

[76] Most of the information on the church comes from a booklet, "The Church of the Assumption," published by the sister of one of the major pastors, Dianne Cicero.

[77] I attended this feast at my grandparents' house at 61 North Main St several times. The head cook was my uncle, Joe, aided by many women from the community who either made the dishes at their homes, or worked with Joe in a kitchen he had set up in the garage.

[78] At this writing I still don't have the official date of purchase. Previous census records locate them at Eagle Street and at 61 Mills street, which is in the same neighborhood, but was considered the "poorer" section even by the Italian community in Mount Morris.

[79] Not documented. But I remember this stove from my early youth. It may have seemed huge by comparison with me

[80] My Aunt Frances referred to this in her recorded interview

[81] No documentation on this, but an assumption given the rapid adoption of this new appliance.

[82] The destruction of his relationship with Liomi detailed earlier. [83] Wikipedia: "It is widely believed that during Christopher Columbus ' first expedition to the New World, San Salvador Island was the first land he sighted and visited on 12 October 1492; he named it *San Salvador* after Christ the Saviour." See: https://en.wikipedia.org/wiki/San_Salvador_Island

[84] Incident related by Frances Guarino in taped interview

[85] From Frances interview. She stayed with that company until she was fifty-two (with ten years off to have and raise her kids).

[86] My speculation

[87] From Frances interview

[88] My speculation

[89] Frances interview

[90] 1920s slang

[91] Slang for strait-laced woman

[92] Because fuel oil is an organic substance, it's a growing medium for certain algae and bacteria. Contaminated oil could impair the engines and piping. Fuel tanks must be carefully cleaned, a process usually done at sea where the contaminated oil could be dumped into the water without any witnesses. Dr. Josh Smith of the American Merchant Marine Museum in King's Point, NY wrote me: "The tanks would be cleaned out periodically to get rid of sludge, etc. Very often this was done with steam, creating a toxic mix of sludge and water that would be pumped overboard—but not while in a harbor!"

[93] I have no idea if this is possible, but it sounds plausible.

[94] This is the only part of the story that's true. All Carmelo said was that they got money from the captain to buy shoes. Only shoes, not whose shoes.

[95] OB is a rank below AB, Carmelo's rank.

[96] There is this documentation from Marine Engineer and Naval Architect - Volume 47 - Page 347
"The Faleria.' We give below an interesting account of an explosion which occurred recently to the main steam stop valve ... Mr. Young's observations are: 'At 9 a.m. on the morning of February 21, 1924, a terrific explosion occurred on board ...'"

[97] My speculation

[98] My speculation

[99] Joan's stepfather, Fred

[100] See: http://www.usccb.org/beliefs-and-teachings/how-we-teach/new-evangelization/jubilee-of-mercy/the-corporal-works-of-mercy.cfm

[101] Related to me by my sister, Mary, recollecting what Nellie had told her

[102] There is such a scene

[103] Involved in an ugly scandal. See: http://crimeinthe1920s.weebly.com/the-fatty-arbuckle-scandal.html

104 See earlier note from Dr. Josh Smith of the American Merchant Marine Museum and the normal procedures for cleaning diesel fuel tanks.

[105] A Roman Catholic doctrine centered on the mother of Jesus. See Wikipedia entry

[106] From interview with Frances Guarino. Her daughter, my cousin, Charlotte, says that when Ms. Macaluso eventually became a nun, she visited Mount Morris several times but she never noticed a shortened limb. Corrective shoes might have masked the condition.

[107] The following accounts, including names, come from the Frances Guarino interview

[108] A Mr. Tate from Rochester was mentioned in the Frances Guarino interview, though no details were given. His first name is invented by me. Note: my brother, Bart, was originally named Richard, but my mother was forced to change it to her father's name, Americanized as Bartholomew. To this day he has two birth certificates, one for each name.

[109] Frances Guarino interview states that Nellie rejected him because of this. The only reason I can imagine is that if he was born with the condition it might indicate another genetic flaw that could afflict her children. Of course, that's the condition I attributed to him here

[110] The Oil Pollution Act of 1924 https://www.revolvy.com/topic/

Oil%20Pollution%20Act%20of%201924

[111] Thanks to my friend, David Johnson, for legal clarification

[112] Adjusted for inflation, $2,500.00 in 1925 is equal to $36,300 in 2019

[113] The name Stogies was a brand at the time, but eventually became generic for "cigars." See: https://www.famous-smoke.com/cigaradvisor/what-are-stogies

[114] A Batavia personage of some repute

[115] Baltimore slang for policeman

[116] See: https://en.wikipedia.org/wiki/St._Leo%27s_Church

[117] Last name of my scoutmaster

[118] True

[119] His original name in Italy was Nino, but everyone in our family knew him as Tony, which was a common male name for immigrant Italians who were routed "To NY" at Ellis Island.

[120] My speculation

[121] According to a 1999 letter from his daughter, Leonarda Grasso Fraker

[122] An invented character

[123] No corroboration

[124] My speculation

[125] Fennel. Carmelo planted lots of it in his garden on Ellicott Street

[126] Based on title of historical novel Westward Ho! "The title of the book derives from the traditional call of boat-taxis on the River Thames, which would call "Eastward ho!" and "Westward ho!" to show their destination." See https://en.wikipedia.org/wiki/Westward_Ho!_(novel) Obviously, I've added a more local context.

[127] The relationship is my speculation. Francy really was the wife of Sebastiano's uncle, Tony.

[128] A documented practice

[129] Per 1940 Census. Equivalent to $13,500 in 2018 dollars. Below

the poverty line, if there was such a thing in 1940.

[130] My speculation. Carmelo lived at 233 Swan Street, which was only a few blocks away from the store at 89.

[131] Fictional character, but name of a former teacher at Joan's boarding school

[132] Comment by Nellie's sister, Frances Guarino, in recorded interview

[133] Joe was a teenager at the time

[134] There's a newspaper item listing him as a musician in the Mount Morris high school band.

[135] Mentioned in Frances Guarino recording

[136] A news story in the *Batavia Daily News* for October 1938 tells of this incident. I've changed the names to correspond to my story. These two young women were listed as bridesmaids at Nellie's wedding the following year. Why she had such young attendants, I don't know, unless they were the only ones available on short notice.

[137] Real name of the car owner was Fuhry. Halsey is my daughter-in-law's family name

[138] The Recchios lived on this street (pronunciation per Carmen)

[139] Short for The Perry Knitting Mill

[140] A longtime police officer, mentioned in the news story.

[141] Mentioned in the news story

[142] A real guy, but probably not connected with the incident or the women. I think his mother was friends with my mother

[143] Quoting friend Neil's grandfather

[144] A pork luncheon meat

[145] A luncheon meat

[146] According the newspaper account

[147] I have a photo of him with this car

[148] A bus line that ran until 1958

[149] My speculation

[150] From Frances Guarino interview

[151] Invented character

[152] From recorded interview

[153] True. She died when she was three.

[154] They married, had three kids, and divorced

[155] Pastor from 1934-1941

[156] Fr. Grasso was born in 1906, making him in his mid-thirties at this point, only four years older than Nellie

[157] Nellie had two sex-ed booklets that I kept for several years, but have lost track of them. I'm speculating she was given them by a priest or some other counselor

[158] Cited in several places. Here's one: co.jp/culture/2018/10/07/ books/haruki-murakami/#.XJTgZy2ZMWo

Sicilian Gothic

The Convergence of Carmelo and Nellie

A novel based on the lives of my parents

Mario Tosto

67292588R00112

Made in the USA
Columbia, SC
25 July 2019